W9-AZR-847

ABOUT THE AUTHOR

With over eight million copies of her books in print worldwide, Barbara Bretton enjoys a warm place in the hearts of romance readers everywhere. After thirty-plus contemporary and historical novels, this bestselling author is listed in *Foremost Women in the Twentieth Century*, and has been honored with numerous writing awards, including *Romantic Times* Reviewer's Choice awards and a Silver Pen Award from *Affaire de Coeur*. Barbara is a two-time nominee for *Romantic Times* Storyteller of the Year. She loves to hear from her readers, who can reach her at: P.O. Box 482, Belle Mead, NJ 08502.

Books by Barbara Bretton

Barbara Bretton

OPERATION:
HUSBAND

Harlequin Books

TORONTO • NEW YORK • LONDON
AMSTERDAM • PARIS • SYDNEY • HAMBURG
STOCKHOLM • ATHENS • TOKYO • MILAN
MADRID • WARSAW • BUDAPEST • AUCKLAND

For Debra Matteucci, for sentimental reasons.
You are, quite simply the best.

ISBN 0-373-16581-1

OPERATION: HUSBAND

Copyright © 1995 by Barbara Bretton.

Prologue

What wound did ever heal but by degrees?
—William Shakespeare

Two years ago—
somewhere near the South China Sea

The last thing Trask Benedict heard before he died was the sound of the bullet that killed him.

They said you never heard the one that had your name on it, but they were wrong. He'd heard it, all right, and he hadn't been all that impressed. A pop, like the kind you heard coming from a kid's cap pistol. A whistling sound in the air around him. His breath rushing from his lungs in a loud and liquid *whoosh.*

One minute he was congratulating himself on getting out of there in one piece, and the next minute he was lying flat out on the deck of a tramp steamer while his blood pooled around him like a Jackson Pollock painting and there wasn't one damn thing he could do about it. He'd always been able to talk himself out of bad situations. He'd flatter, cajole, threaten, say whatever he had to say to get his own way, then turn around and nail the unlucky bastard dumb enough to let him get the upper hand.

It was one of the things PAX liked best about him.

There hadn't been a boardroom, bedroom, or back room that stayed closed to him for long. It always amazed him the amount of information you could accumulate with nothing more than a quick brain, a fast mouth and a killer grin.

Except this time.

The Kevlar vest.

The thought came to him slowly, too slowly to matter. He'd left the bulletproof vest back at the hotel. You only needed a vest if you believed something could happen to you, and Trask had always believed he would live forever. The man with a wife and two kids and a mortgage to pay—that was the guy who had to worry about the future.

Trask had nothing worth living for. Insurance policies didn't come any better than that.

He tried to laugh as they gathered around him, talking loud and fast in a language he used to understand but no longer did. He saw their mouths moving, but couldn't hear the words. All he heard was the soft pop of that bullet, over and over again.

Why were they standing there, wringing their hands together? There was nothing they could do. Nothing anyone could do. He'd been dodging that bullet his entire life, and it had finally found him here on the other side of the world.

The night sky grew darker above him, then suddenly lifted, like the rag top of his old Mustang convertible, exposing the brilliant blue sky of his childhood. Lemon yellow sun gilded emerald blades of grass, the colors achingly pure and true.

His mother waited up on the crest of the hill. She was young and pretty, her fair hair pulled back with a tortoiseshell clip, the way she'd worn it when he was a child. The castle where she'd grown up rose up proud and majestic behind her. Had she ever smiled at him that way, as if she were glad to see him? His father was there, too, tall and strong and in his prime. *"Come on, son. We've been waiting for you."*

They hadn't had time for him in life, but now they were eager for his company. He wondered if this was his heaven or their hell.

He started toward them, but it was like walking through a sea of cotton candy. Five steps. Ten. No matter how many steps he took, he couldn't bridge the distance between them. The low rumble of their laughter rode toward him on a wave of memory.

He broke into a run. Slow at first, then faster, gaining speed but not distance. His lungs ached with every breath. Damn it, he was dead. Nothing was supposed to hurt when you were dead.

"Trask."

He hesitated. That voice. That sweet voice. He tried to focus through a gathering haze.

"I love you," she said. *"I've never stopped loving you."*

She stood not five feet from him, her long, dark hair tangled about her delicate shoulders. She smelled of jasmine and innocence, of half-forgotten dreams. They'd had less than two weeks together, but those ten days had been the stuff of dreams.

This isn't real, he told himself. She was back in Houston, back on the other side of the world. She probably had a husband and children by now, a family to love instead of him.

But she had loved him.

Once, a long time ago, she'd loved him, and that had almost been enough to save him.

He stumbled, barely saving himself from a fall. Was he going crazy, or had the sun grown dimmer?

He stumbled again. This time he fell heavily, landing on his right knee. The pain was white-hot. Vicious. Almost as bad as the dark and heavy pain crushing its way out from his rib cage, choking off his breath, his life.

Houston, Texas—three days later

THE ENCRYPTED MESSAGE came in a little after midnight. Lucky Wilde snapped instantly awake at the sound of electronic machinery receiving a message from headquarters. It had been a long time since one of these late-night missives had come his way, and an even longer time since he'd been part of the PAX infrastructure. Slowly he was working his way out of the organization, back into the rarefied atmosphere of the real world.

He switched on the light next to his bed and fumbled around for his eyeglasses. He'd been feeling puny lately, not like himself at all. His friend Ted, a cardiologist, wanted to run some of those dad-blamed tests fancy doctors were so fond of, but Lucky was holding firm. There was nothing wrong with him that a few days out at the ranch wouldn't cure.

He slid the glasses on. They settled automatically into the deep grooves on either side of the bridge of his nose. To hell with slippers, he thought as he swung his legs from the bed. Might as well live dangerously.

The equipment was kept in a locked safe at the back of his dressing room. Everyone thought that was where he stashed away the best jewels Wilde & Daughters had to offer their finest customers: fancy yellow diamonds in platinum settings, Burmese rubies, Russian alexandrite stones big as robins' eggs. Better they went on believing that. The truth was a hell of a lot more dangerous.

Sometimes he wondered how it was he'd managed all those years with three bright, inquisitive daughters in the house. It had been easy enough to explain away occasional business trips to exotic places with strange-sounding names when they were young, but as they grew older, he'd found it more difficult to find excuses for the middle-of-the-night phone calls, locked rooms and prolonged absences.

And impossible to condone the fact that he was putting his beloved girls at risk.

The safe was conveniently set at eye level. He punched in his access code, waited a moment, then peered through the eyepiece for retinal identification. Another moment passed, then another. Finally he heard a series of clicks as, one by one, the locks tumbled open. He swung open the safe and pulled out the encryption machine. Pressing the glowing red button on the right side, he said his name out loud and waited for a voice ID. Seconds later, the button glowed green and a sheet of paper slid from the opening on top.

TERMINATION NOTICE

NAME: Benedict, Trask
AGE: 34
BIRTHPLACE: Newport, Rhode Island
FAMILY: None
HEIGHT: 6'3"   **WEIGHT:** 185 lbs.
HAIR: Brown   **EYES:** Hazel
SERVICE HISTORY: Europe, Southeast Asia, the Middle East. Situation in Cairo handled successfully but cleanup necessary. A loner. Loyalties uncertain.
CURRENT STATUS: KIA aboard Portuguese steamer "The Orient Queen." Body returned to Honolulu for burial. Terminate payroll #890322XKY.

Sorry, Lucky. I know he was one of yours.
Ryder O'Neal

LUCKY'S EYES BURNED, and he felt a tightness in his chest. He hated death, hated it with his entire heart and soul. He'd seen so much of it along the way, blamed himself for half of it, even if there'd been nothing he could do to stop the inevitable. Sometimes when he was overtired and the sweet oblivion of sleep wouldn't come, he thought of his second wife, Marta, and all the ways in which he'd failed her.

She'd been younger than Trask when she died in a plane crash, and Lucky had never quite gotten over missing her, not even now, after two decades.

He stared down at the paper. Thirty-four years old. Hell, that was just the blink of an eye. He'd still been wet behind the ears at that age, struggling to turn his daddy's little jewelry store into a force to be reckoned with. You were just getting started in your thirties, flexing your muscles, figuring out how you were going to make your dreams come true.

He folded the paper and put it back in the safe, then locked the door again. Other people had said Trask Benedict wouldn't make it over the long haul, that he burned too bright and too carelessly. Lucky had defended his protégé. "Sure he makes mistakes, but damned if he doesn't always come through."

Except this time.

Lucky should have known better. The odds had been against Trask from the beginning. With few exceptions, it was never the flashy James Bond types who made a go of it. It was the nondescript team players who would wait patiently for ten years to show their cards and then were willing to fold, if that was what they were told to do.

Nothing wrong with being a team player. The world needed more of them, if it was going to get out of the mess it was in. A smart man knew there was only room for one lead sled dog on a team.

His eyes filled with tears. "Damnation," he swore softly as years of regret settled across his shoulders. Had he made a mistake? Trask and his daughter Martie had been all wrong for each other. A wild young man and a sheltered girl who didn't understand that the human heart was made to be broken. Had it been wrong to put a stop to it before either one of them got hurt?

A bitter laugh rose in his throat and he wished he had a brandy to wash it back down. *Before either one of them got hurt.* Trask was dead. Martie was alone. And life grew colder and darker with every day that passed.

A tightness spread across his chest, and he absently rubbed his shoulder. Sometimes he swore he could hear the ticking of a clock, counting down the hours and minutes of his life. It goes so fast, he thought, as the tightness grew heavier. Blink your eyes and the end is staring you in the face.

He thought about his three girls. Sam and Frankie would manage. They both had themselves more self-confidence than the law allowed. It wasn't hard to see that those two apples hadn't fallen very far from the family tree.

Martie was different. His middle girl had been blessed with beauty and brains and a talent so rare that it bordered on genius. Her innovative jewelry designs had sparked a revolution at Wilde & Daughters Ltd. that had now spread from Houston to Milan. Hell, in the last year, her lovely face and exquisite designs had graced more magazine covers than he could count.

Ask anybody and they'd tell you that Martina Wilde had the world by the tail, so why was it she was still alone? Why did she go home at night to that empty guest cottage, instead of to a man who loved her, children who needed her—the things that were real and lasting in this foolish world?

You know why, old man, Lucky thought as he climbed back into bed. He'd known it for ten years . . . since the night he'd told his daughter that the man she loved was dead.

And now it was true.

The bitter taste of regret filled his mouth, and he lay back against the pillows and took its full measure. He shifted, trying to find a comfortable position, but there was none to be had. Not ever. Secretly he had always prayed they would find each other again, that the world would straighten itself out and become a place that cherished goodness and love. But now it was too late.

Trask was dead, and Martie was only going through the motions, living a half-life that grew more brittle with every day that passed.

She deserved more than that. She deserved the richness of a home of her own, a husband and family.

He'd played God once, with dismal results, but he'd learned from his mistakes. This time it would all be different.

He placed his eyeglasses on the night table, and shut off the light. Even though it was too late, he whispered a prayer for Trask Benedict, and then he said one for his daughter and for himself.

He prayed their luck would hold.

THEN

How often things occur by mere chance which
we dare not even hope for.
—Terence

Chapter One

Martina Wilde hated parties, loud rock and big crowds—in that order—which made the night of her seventeenth birthday one of the worst in recorded history.

If her father, Lucky, had tried to devise a better form of torture, he would have had to consult with Vlad the Impaler to come up with something that could top this.

The big house swarmed with people this April night. Scores of her father's friends filled the ballroom, laughing and flirting and pretending they were seventeen again, which, as far as Martie was concerned, was not a pretty sight when you were sixty years old, with liver spots the size of mushrooms.

Oh, her friends were there, too, but they didn't even begin to make a dent in the crowd. She wasn't like her sisters Sam and Frankie, who had tons of friends who called them on the phone and asked them out to parties and movies and football games. Not that Martie would have gone to any of them, you understand, but it would have been nice to have the chance to say no. There was power in the word *no*, more power than most people realized. Say yes and automatically you were one of the crowd, another sheep in a herd of sheep in search of a new pasture to graze in. All you had to do was say no, and the fences tumbled and the whole wide world opened up before you, all shiny and new and waiting to be discovered.

"Hey, Martie!" Billy Taylor, clutching a can of beer, waved at her from the other side of the room. "Happy birthday!" Billy and Sam had been dating since junior high, though, for the life of her, Martie couldn't figure out what her sister saw in the prelaw student. Not that there was anything wrong with him. Billy was a nice enough guy and pleasant to look at, but he didn't make her heart beat faster.

Even Frankie, the youngest of the three Wilde girls, thought Billy was a major catch. Of course, Frankie was only fourteen, but that still didn't explain the fact that when it came to men, Martie just didn't understand what every other female in Texas seemed to know from the cradle onward.

Sometimes she thought it was because she was adopted and not Lucky's biological child at all. She'd been told her birth parents were both New

Yorkers, and maybe that northern blood had skewed her perceptions, dooming her to be a bystander when it came to romance.

It seemed as good an explanation as any other she'd been able to come up with.

She wanted... Oh, she didn't know what she wanted. She couldn't find a name for it, wasn't even sure if there *was* a name for the emotions inside her heart. Sometimes, right there in the middle of her loud and loving family, she felt so lonely she couldn't breathe, like she was watching life happen all around her while she stood waiting for something—anything—to happen to her.

And she couldn't talk about it with any of them. They'd never understand. Her father and sisters were cut from the same bolt of cloth, the weave and color all even, while Martie was a patchwork quilt. Lucky and her sisters saw the world the way it was; Martie saw it the way she wanted it to be. Reality rarely made a dent in her consciousness, except to remind her of all the wonderful things that remained just beyond her grasp.

She wanted excitement. She wanted to be swept away by desire. She wanted to live on the edge of her emotions, to know how it felt to love someone so much that she would risk everything to be by his side. She wanted to be dizzy with longing, alive with possibilities, certain that destiny had something splendid planned for her.

"I felt that way at seventeen," Estelle, head gemstone buyer for Wilde & Daughters Ltd., had said with a rueful shake of her head. "Trust me. You'll get over it."

I don't want to get over it, Martie thought as she watched business tycoons elbow society columnists for space on the dance floor. Getting over it would mean she'd grown old and complacent, too jaded and cynical to believe in the wonders of love.

Because deep inside she was the real romantic in the family. Frankie and Sam might be world-class flirts, but they were as practical as the day was long. No one had ever called Martie practical.

She edged her way toward the door. The music was loud, and so was the laughter. People were having themselves a grand time, drinking Lucky's booze and eating his food, and maybe only a handful of them even remembered the reason they were here.

Not that she cared. She didn't want to be here in the first place, she thought as she climbed the stairs. Tucked away on the third floor was her magic room, the place where she left the boring, everyday world behind and slipped into her dreams.

The third-floor roof was sharply pitched, but she was so tiny that it didn't matter, and she hurried down the hallway toward her oasis. She unlocked the door, then carefully made her way through the dark room until she found the desk lamp. A soft, rosy glow softened the edges of the stark attic room, and she smiled, delighted to be in her favorite place on earth.

The cleaning staff referred to the room as the Forbidden Zone, because Martie wouldn't let them so much as polish the padlock on the door, but she didn't care. Once she closed that door behind her, the world dropped away. There, spread out on the scarred surface of the wooden worktable, was the stuff of dreams.

Small nuggets of gold and silver that might have once belonged to a queen or a sorcerer. Mine-cut diamonds and cushion-cut sapphires from the pieces her mother had left to her. And her precious collection of jeweler's tools that had once belonged to Lucky, all lined up neatly on a piece of black velvet.

Her breath caught in her throat when she noticed the basket sitting on the window ledge.

Heart pounding, she crossed the room to the window and peered into the basket. Uncut peridots, the clear green of early spring, glittered next to chunks of vivid pink morganite, still unpolished, and oval turquoise, flecked with fool's gold, that might once have helped a pharaoh to find favor with the gods.

And, best of all, a bouquet of zircons in a shade of blue so saturated with light and intensity that it stole her breath away, powerful stones, imbued with the wisdom of the centuries.

Leave it to Lucky to know exactly what would make her birthday complete.

She held one of the stones in the palm of her hand, relishing its coolness and weight, trying to absorb its magic through her pores. Legend said zircons could banish grief and sadness from a man's heart, and she believed it. There was magic and wonder in the fruits of the inner earth, but you had to open up your own heart to give the magic room to grow.

In her mind's eye, she saw a ring of burnished gold, and in the center of that ring was an unpolished zircon of the deepest blue. She couldn't see the man who would be worthy of such a gift, but she knew he was out there. He'd been hurt somehow, and badly, but she didn't think he had been hurt by a woman. No, the pain went even deeper, as if the center of his being had been under attack for so long that he no longer remembered how it felt to believe in goodness.

And she loved him. It didn't matter that she'd never met him, that she didn't know his face or the sound of his voice or the feel of his mouth against hers.

Some nights she lay awake in her bed, listening to the wild beating of her heart, knowing that one day she'd turn a corner and he would be there and it would be like coming home to a place she'd never been.

THE OLD MAN had told him to stay in the guest house while the party was going on, but Trask Benedict had never been one to play by the rules. Hell, if he'd been good at playing by the rules, he wouldn't be there in the first place, learning the tricks of the trade from one of the acknowledged masters of the game.

Six months ago, Trask had been bumming around Europe, doing his best to spend his inheritance and alienate as many foreign cultures as he could. Single-handedly he'd managed to resurrect the image of the ugly American, and he'd been on his way to becoming an incarcerated American when Lucky Wilde found him.

Actually, Trask was the one who'd found Lucky. He'd pretty much exhausted the London club scene, and the wreck of a castle where his mother had grown up as part of the declining English aristocracy hadn't provided much in the way of excitement. He'd been looking for a new way to get his kicks when he hit on the idea of picking pockets. He didn't need the money, but he did need the excitement. If he wasn't out there on the edge, he was nowhere, and nowhere was the first place the demons looked.

He spotted the guy in a restaurant near Budapest. He might as well have had the American flag sewn onto the back of his hand-tailored suit. The guy was too big and brawny to be anything but.

Probably carried a big fat wallet in his back pocket, just waiting to be snagged.

He'd been right about the nationality, but wrong about the wallet. It was big and fat, all right, but the second Trask made his move, the old man sprang to life, pinning him to the floor of the restaurant, while the owner called the authorities.

"Big mistake," the old man drawled. Just Trask's luck to jump a Texan. "The police here don't take too kindly to stunts like this."

"Go to hell," Trask snarled, trying to escape his grasp.

"Soon enough," the old man said with a laugh. "But first we're gonna talk."

That had been six months ago. Turned out Wilde had been on his tail since Vienna, waiting for him to screw up bad enough for him to step in and clean up the mess. Lucky was an old friend of Trask's late parents. He'd designed Lillian Benedict's engagement and wedding rings, and the silver cup that had celebrated Trask's birth. When he'd heard someone talking about the American kid with the penchant for getting in trouble, he'd quickly discovered Trask's identity and set out to save his sorry ass.

All of which amounted to less than nothing, as far as Trask was concerned. His ass didn't need saving, no matter what Wilde might think. Who gave a damn about some rich jeweler who traveled around Europe buying diamonds and hobnobbing with royalty?

Trask knew the type. You send your kids off to boarding school as soon as they're out of diapers, then sell them in marriage to the highest bidder. The upper-middle-class American way of child-rearing. No muss. No fuss. Except when you wrote out a check to the nanny and headmaster, your hands never got dirty.

But Lucky Wilde was different. He'd brought up his three girls alone, and never once had he given in to the urge to ship them off to school and let someone else worry about them. After his second wife died, when their youngest was four years old, Lucky had thrown himself headlong into fatherhood, and he'd never once looked back. Now—for some strange reason—he'd turned that same parental intensity on Trask.

And, damn it, Trask liked it. Even though he was twenty-two years old and an adult in the eyes of the world, there was a part of him that was still a kid looking for approval from parents who had been too busy enjoying life to care whether their son was screwing up his own.

Lucky had not only kept the Hungarian authorities off his tail, he'd taken Trask under his considerable wing.

"You're a hothead," Lucky had said, "but that's all right. I'll teach you how to channel that anger."

Nothing would change Trask into an even-tempered, careful type, but Lucky was opening up a world to him that not even a kid born with a silver spoon in his mouth had ever imagined. Lucky's life in Houston was about money and power and privilege, the holy trinity of the American dream. His life away from Houston was about power, too, but power such as few people on earth could understand.

This can be yours was the unspoken message. A life lived not just in the fast lane, but outside the natural order of things.

"We'll start slow," Lucky had told him when they flew into Houston last night from the preliminary-training center in northeastern Connecticut. "If you make the cut, you'll be sent to Anchorage for more intensive training."

Trask had laid his hand against the left side of his rib cage, where a tiny transmitter chip had been embedded. "I didn't know you were going to wire me for sound."

"There's a lot you don't know," Lucky said with his booming laugh. "But you'll learn, son. You'll learn."

Of course, they hadn't wired him only for sound. That microchip was an electronic leash, meant to harness him to the PAX machinery in ways he didn't even know about yet.

But, damn it, he wanted to know. He hummed with anger and reckless energy, and if Lucky didn't get things rolling soon, he would take matters into his own hands. Didn't they get it? He understood the risks and he embraced them. If they thought they were going to scare him away, they were wrong. He had no friends or family to worry about him, nobody to mourn him if he bought the farm in some foreign hellhole. If he wanted to risk his neck going where sane men refused to venture, it was his business.

All he needed was for Lucky Wilde to give him the go-ahead, and the sky was the limit.

The sounds of music and laughter floated up the staircase from the main ballroom. There'd been a ballroom in his parents' house, too, but they'd never stayed home long enough to use it. No, they'd always been on the move, jetting to Paris or driving down to New York, in search of the ultimate experience.

They'd finally found that ultimate experience eight years ago on a small road near Cap d'Antibes, when their rented Ferrari slid down an embankment and into the blue waters of the Mediterranean.

He didn't think about his parents very often. Why should he? They hadn't thought much about him when they were alive. People wasted too much time thinking about things they couldn't change. He wasn't about to make that mistake.

The first floor of Lucky's house was off-limits while the party was going on. If the old man caught him snooping, he'd probably pull some strings and send his butt back to Hungary and a jail sentence.

The second floor was a drag. Lucky had a suite of rooms in the east wing, with lots of wood and cowboy artwork on the walls, fierce paintings that smelled like dust and blood, a far cry from the discreet watercolors of Trask's childhood.

Lucky's daughters' rooms were in the west wing. They all looked alike to Trask, with lots of flowery wallpaper, fancy furniture, and every kind of electronic gadget available. The shelves sagged with CD players, headphones, computer equipment, televisions, and plain old garden-variety radios. Two of the rooms even had the same frilly white curtains billowing across the windows.

The third room, however, was different. It boasted no curtains at all. Instead, the windows were bare, large rectangles of glass and wood that looked out over a small lake backed by a stand of pine trees. But it wasn't the view that caught his eye. Polished stones in all different sizes and shapes lined the sill, purples and blues and greens, as pure as spring. A crystal in the shape of a teardrop spun from a golden chain, glittering in the moonlight.

He stood for a moment, transfixed. The scent of flowers filled the air, light and sweet and hauntingly unfamiliar, and a strange stirring began deep in his gut that was unlike anything he'd ever felt before.

He didn't particularly like the feeling—it made him aware of the chinks in his armor—and abruptly he turned away and headed for the back stairs that led to the third floor. There wasn't much to see there, either, mostly a lot of small, square rooms that were used for storage. He was about to go back downstairs when he noticed a light burning in the last room at the end of the hall. Probably more of the same, he thought, or maybe a maid's room.

Still, something tugged at his curiosity, and he found himself drawn toward the light.

The door was partly open. A young girl of seventeen or eighteen sat at the far end of a long table, staring intently at a pair of huge gold earrings. Her dark hair spilled across her fragile shoulders like a blanket of silk. She wore a shimmery white dress that hugged her breasts and fit snugly at her waist. The skirt was short and swingy, stopping well above her knees, leaving the slender length of her legs bare. She had a delicate heart-shaped face, fair skin, and wide, innocent aqua eyes that weren't like any eyes he'd ever seen before.

She turned the earrings over in her hand, in a gesture of artless sensuality that moved along his skin like an electrical charge.

His heart seemed to swell inside his chest as he watched her. He'd heard about love at first sight, but he knew he was too cynical and jaded for something as miraculous as that. But still there was a pull, a tug of something deep inside the emptiness he called a heart that even he couldn't deny.

"Which one are you?" he asked, making sure he sounded like he didn't much give a damn. "You're Frankie, right?"

Her gaze was as direct as her father's. "Frankie's the youngest and the prettiest. Sam's the oldest and the smartest."

He grinned. She was everything he'd hoped, and more. "And that makes you..."

"Martie," she said in a husky voice. "The one everybody forgets."

Chapter Two

The stranger leaned against the doorjamb, left thumb hooked through his belt loop, and grinned at her, and Martie forgot how to breathe. Her heart seemed too big for her chest, yet too small for the violent emotions that were growing stronger with each second that passed.

She knew she shouldn't stare at him, but beauty moved her the way nothing else could, and he was the most beautiful man she'd ever seen. He had a swimmer's body: broad chest and shoulders, narrow waist, long muscular legs. He wore jeans and a T-shirt and a pair of cowboy boots that had seen better days. His hair was dark brown, streaked in spots by the sun, and it hadn't seen a pair of barber's scissors in a long time.

But it was his face that caught and held her eye. His glorious, angelic face. He had a full, well-defined mouth, a strong jaw, and hazel eyes that met hers with a challenge she couldn't resist. It wasn't fair that a man be so perfect, so splendid, that looking at him brought tears of wonder to her eyes, but he was exactly that.

You're the one, she thought, stunned by the knowledge. *You're the man I love.*

SOMETHING was happening to him. Trask felt as if his heart had been cracked open wide and all his dreams laid bare in front of her eyes.

He didn't want to feel this way. He'd spent the past twenty-four years protecting his heart by denying its existence, and with one look this girl had stripped him bare.

He hated her for it, hated her innocence and how that innocence reminded him of all he'd lost along the way, of all he'd never had. But, damn her, he couldn't turn away. The pull between them was too strong. The need inside him, too great.

"Who are you?" she asked, pushing her heavy hair off her face. A silver ring glittered from the index finger of her left hand. A trio of shiny bracelets sparkled from her right wrist. He wondered if she believed in magic. "What are you doing up here on the third floor?" She sounded edgy, slightly defensive. He couldn't blame her. This was her house, and he was a stranger.

The name Lucky had told him to use vanished. "I'm Trask Benedict."

"Trask Benedict," she repeated. He'd never liked his name before. When she said it, it sounded like a love song. "Never heard of you."

"I've heard of you," he said. "Your old man talks a lot about you and your sisters."

Her cheeks reddened slightly, but she didn't soften her tone. "What are you doing here? We don't allow strangers above the first floor."

"You and the White House," he drawled.

She glared at him. "I'm not going to ask you again," she warned, reaching for the intercom button on the wall next to her.

"Don't!" He stepped forward. "It's okay. I'm with your old man."

"Right," she said with a laugh. "I suppose you always wear jeans to a formal party."

"I wasn't invited to the party," he admitted.

Her silky dark brows lifted. "So you decided to crash it?"

He had to be careful. Lucky's daughters knew nothing of their old man's involvement with PAX. Lucky had made it clear that Trask would be history if he compromised his family in any way.

"I work for your father."

"Doing what?"

She was as single-minded as her old man. "I'm helping him out with a project."

"What project?"

"You ask a lot of questions."

"Yes," she said, "and I like answers."

"Do you screen all of your old man's employees?"

"When I get the chance." Her eyes twinkled. "So what are you doing for Daddy?"

"I'm wiring the guest house for sound." It was the only thing he could think of to say.

"The guest house? Nobody's stayed in the guest house since my mom died."

She fell silent, watching him carefully, and he felt it again, that sense of something bigger than himself, something bigger than either one of them could ever hope to be.

"Why would Daddy put in a sound system when nobody uses the guest house?"

"Maybe he's going to take in boarders." He shot her a grin that hid the deep emotions growing inside his chest. "I don't ask questions, Princess. I just cash my paycheck."

She considered him for a few moments, then nodded. He almost felt guilty. He wondered how Lucky had managed it all these years, living in two different worlds. Could he even tell the difference anymore?

"You're staring at me."

"I'm looking at the earrings," he said, which was partly true. "They'd look great on you."

Her face lit up with a smile, and he felt as if someone had just handed him a million dollars.

"You like them?" she asked, sounding terribly pleased.

"Yeah," he said, taking a good look at the earrings, and then at her small, perfect ears. "I like the way they catch the light."

She tossed the earrings to him, and he caught them in the palm of his right hand. The warmth of the yellow metal surprised him. Three heavy bands of burnished gold had been braided together, then twisted to form a knot the size of a baby's fist. Instead of their seeming garish, the effect was one of warmth and understated elegance.

He tossed them back to her. "Put them on."

She shook her head, that high color again staining her cheeks.

"Go on," he urged, turning on the charm. "They look like they were made for you."

"They were," she said. "I'm the one who made them."

"You're kidding."

She shook her head. "No, I'm not. I designed these myself."

"Right," he said, going along with the joke. "You just happened to have a nugget of gold lying around, and you whipped up a pair of earrings."

"Something like that."

Suddenly the rest of the room came into sharp focus. Precious metals gleamed in the lamplight. Strange-looking tools rested on a strip of black velvet cloth. Design sketches were thumbtacked to every available surface. "Damn," he said with admiration. "You're good."

SHE KNEW that he didn't understand one blessed thing about jewelry and probably wouldn't know sterling from sheet metal, but still his words pleased her.

"Thanks," she said, ducking her head. "I have a lot to learn."

"Not that much," he said, stepping closer to the worktable. "People would pay good money for this stuff."

She tilted her chin slightly as she met his eyes. "I sold my first piece last month," she announced, unable to mask her pride. "And not to a relative."

"So you do have a sense of humor," he said. "I was beginning to wonder."

"I have a particularly well-developed sense of the absurd," she said, grinning. "All Texans do." She fiddled with a length of bismark chain, praying he wouldn't notice the ridiculous way her hands were shaking. "Where are you from?"

"Rhode Island," he said.

"You're kidding."

"Something wrong with Rhode Island?"

"It's . . . small."

"So are you."

"I'm petite," she countered. "There's a difference."

"Make something for me," he said. "I want to watch you work."

"No." She pushed her hair off her face. "I never let anyone watch me."

"Make an exception."

"Absolutely not."

He reached for one of the uncut blue zircons she had lined up along the edge of the worktable. Her breath caught in her throat as he rolled the stone around in the palm of his hand. She wished she were the zircon.

She reached for a knot of heavy, lustrous silver. The idea was fuzzy, more an impression than anything else, but she'd learned to trust herself.

He leaned closer, and his smell made her dizzy with longing. People didn't talk about smell the way they talked about sight and sound. There was something too earthy about the way a person smelled, something dark and unknowable and deeply sensual, that seemed too uncivilized for most people.

He smelled of moonless nights and windswept beaches and a loneliness so deep that she feared her own heart would break from it. She felt as if she'd stepped out of her own skin and crawled into his. Instead of being terrified by the powerful emotions building inside her chest, she felt elated, as if

she'd tapped into a source of energy so elemental
that it couldn't be denied.

TRASK KNEW it was dangerous, but he couldn't tear
his gaze from her mouth. Her lips were full, rosy
pink, and inviting. Made for kissing.

And, damn it, he wanted to kiss her even if she
was his boss's daughter and about as off-limits as
you could get.

She brushed against him once as she reached for
a pair of jeweler's tweezers, and his entire body was
galvanized, yet she didn't seem to realize the effect
she was having on him. She was absorbed in her
work, her movements fluid and graceful, and he
wasn't sure she remembered he was there. A slight
frown pleated her forehead as she patiently shaped
the silver into a bold ring that was more angles than
curves. He'd never seen anything quite like it before, but that shouldn't surprise him, he knew.

He'd never seen anything like her.

The sound of car engines broke the cocoon of silence that surrounded them. Laughter and conversation floated up from the courtyard, mingling with
the rumble of automobiles.

They locked glances across the table. His eyes
were hazel, with golden flecks. The lashes were
thick and dark. *Our children will be beautiful,* she
thought with a rush of fierce exultation. *Strong and
fearless and honorable.*

"Mar-ti-na!" Lucky's voice rang out above the other sounds. "Come down here now!"

The spell broke like shattering glass.

"He's furious," Martie said, glancing toward the window. Worse than that, he was probably embarrassed that the guest of honor hadn't bothered to stay until the end of the party.

Trask looked at her, and they started to laugh. It was the half guilty, half elated laughter of two people who know they've stumbled into something unexpected . . . and wonderful.

"We can't walk downstairs together," Martie said.

"Why not?" he countered. "It's not like we were doing anything."

She blushed furiously. Even the tops of her breasts, exposed by her dress, reddened. "We can't, that's all. Besides, didn't Daddy tell you to wait for him in the guest house? He'll be mad as blazes if you're not there when he shows up."

"So let him get mad," Trask said. He didn't care what the old man thought. Right now, the only thing he cared about was standing there next to her, breathing the air she breathed. "You got a car?"

Her eyes widened. "Sure, I've got a car."

"We could go for a drive."

"You don't care much about your job, do you?"

He grinned. "Not right now, I don't."

Martie could barely contain her joy. This total stranger, this absolutely *gorgeous* total stranger, was willing to risk his job to be with her. Everyone in town knew Lucky was the world's best employer and, judging from his faded jeans and T-shirt, Trask Benedict needed every dollar he stood to make.

She felt as if champagne were racing through her veins, as if she'd just awakened from a long sleep to find herself in a golden land. She'd always been invisible, the middle child sandwiched between two outrageous personalities who demanded attention and invariably got it. She'd been content to stay in the shadows, never quite certain that the love that came her way was meant for her alone.

But this moment, this incredible, magical moment, belonged only to her. *He* belonged to her. She knew it the same way she knew her name.

"So is there a back staircase in this place?"

Laughter bubbled up from somewhere deep inside her. "It leads down to the garage."

"Think we can get out without being seen?"

"I know we can."

He held out his hand to her. She hesitated, knowing that once she touched him there could be no turning back, that from that moment on, every minute, every second, of her life would belong to him.

And then she put her hand in his and stepped out into the unknown.

Chapter Three

She took him to a place north of town, where the lights of the city were only a memory.

Trask lay on his back in the fragrant grass. "Incredible," he said as a shooting star angled across the moon.

"Incredible," she whispered. Not even nature's splendor could come close to matching the wonder of his beautiful face. She longed to press her lips against the underside of his jaw, to trace the proud angles of his cheekbones with her fingertips. To brand him as her own.

Feelings she'd never even imagined were erupting inside her heart, feelings so wild and fierce they stole her breath. She could spend the rest of her life memorizing the way moonlight illuminated his angel's face.

"Don't be fooled," he said. "I'm not a nice guy."

Her cheeks reddened, and she blessed the darkness. "That's a strange thing to say."

"Maybe," he said, "but it's true."

"Why tell me?" she asked, her heartbeat accelerating with sheer delight in danger.

"Because I think you need to hear it."

She ducked her head and let her hair swing over her cheeks, obscuring her face. "So now I know."

He reached up and captured a lock of her hair between two fingers. "I usually get what I want."

She savored the gentle tug against her scalp. "So do I."

He leaned up on one elbow. "I want to kiss you."

"That's what I want you to do," she said as she lay down next to him.

He cupped her face with his hands. His fingertips were rough and callused, but warm—so warm—against her skin. He made a sound low in his throat, then captured her mouth with his, and the last of her defenses crumbled.

She belonged to him.

She always had.

She always would.

SHE WAS SO EAGER, so innocent, so damn beautiful, that he knew he had to stop things before she gave herself to him and he claimed her body the way she'd already claimed his heart.

She lay beneath him on the grass, her sweet young breasts trembling with desire, and he knew the only thing between him and paradise was what remained of his self-control. He slid his hand under her skirt and traced the supple length of her thigh, registering her softness, the silky fabric of her panties, the silky moist heat of her desire. He wanted to bury himself in her body, breathe in her musky female scent, taste her sweetness on his tongue.

He wanted to have her crying out his name as he took her to the height of desire and brought her back to earth again, and then he wanted to do it over and over again.

For the rest of his life.

"WE SHOULD GO HOME." She lay in his arms, hair tousled, lips deliciously swollen from his kisses. They had been together in the grass for hours. "The sun's about to come up."

"Do you want to go home?" He smiled down at her, his hazel eyes crinkling at the outer edges. *Beautiful eyes,* she thought. No one on earth had eyes so kind or so loving.

"I want to stay here forever," she said, pressing kisses along the underside of his jaw.

"You don't have to go back home," he said, and she sensed both delight and danger in his words. "Stay with me."

How she wanted to! How she wanted to forget everything else in the world except this glorious fallen angel of a man! "I have to go home," she said. "Lucky will be worried. I've never stayed out all night before in my life."

"Daddy's little girl," he said, cupping her breasts with his big strong hands. "What would he do if he knew?"

She started to laugh, shy and embarrassed and secretly delighted to have so wicked a secret. "Maybe he'd understand."

"Right," Trask said, laughing, too. "And he'd ask if I wanted to share your room."

"Lucky's an old softie," she said, straightening the bodice of her party dress as she sat up. "No, really!" she protested when she saw Trask's look of utter disbelief. "He talks like an old cowboy, but he's a sucker for a happy ending."

He pulled her against him, so close that she could feel his heart beating inside his chest. She'd read that phrase a thousand times in novels and never quite understood how profound an experience it could be.

"No ending," he said. "Not for this story." He looked deep into her eyes, and she saw straight into his soul. "Not for us."

LUCKY WAS WAITING for them on the front porch when they came home.

"Where in hell have you been?" he roared at his daughter. "I was ready to call the police!"

She lifted her chin and clung to Trask's hand. *Be happy for me, Daddy. I've met the man I'll spend my life with.* "We went for a drive."

"You have a lot of explaining to do, missy." Lucky fixed her with a dark look. There was no amusement in his eyes, no tenderness in his voice. Only anger. "Get some sleep," he ordered. "We'll talk this afternoon."

With that, he turned to Trask, with an intensity that scared Martie. She'd never seen her father like this before, bristling with an anger that seemed to border on fear. Trask met her father's eyes with a challenge of his own, and a delicious ripple of excitement moved along her spine, displacing everything else.

"You and I are going to have us a talk, son," Lucky said to Trask. "A long talk."

"Fine," Trask shot back. "Start talking."

The tension between the two men made the air crackle. She hated the idea of leaving Trask for even a minute.

"Go to your room, Martina." Her father's voice was stern. "I said I'll deal with you later."

She hesitated, but Trask made it easy for her. "I'll be here," he said, and she heard a lifetime of promises in those simple words.

Loud voices followed her as she headed toward the staircase. She hoped Lucky wouldn't fire Trask for slipping away from the party with her. All they had done was drive out to the edge of town and watch the sun come up. They hadn't made love, yet she felt as if they'd somehow pledged their lives to each other.

And they had. She knew they had, even though they hadn't said the words. It was there in his eyes, in his tone of voice, in the way he touched her, as if she were a rare and precious thing.

She paused on the second-floor landing. She couldn't make out the words, but the emotions behind them were crystal-clear. Lucky loved his daughters. He'd been mother and father to them for almost as long as she could remember. It had to be difficult to meet the man who would take your place in your daughter's heart.

Her own heart tightened painfully. Lucky was angry, but he wasn't vindictive. He wouldn't take the job away from Trask. He couldn't.

All you had to do was look at Trask to know he needed the money. His jeans were threadbare, his boots badly scuffed and run down at the heels. There wasn't an extra ounce of flesh on his large frame. She thought about the mountains of food that had gone uneaten at her birthday party and wished she could smuggle some of it out to him in the guest house on the other side of the pine trees.

Considering the fact that Lucky hadn't set foot in there since he lost his wife, Martie found it odd that her father had a sudden desire to wire the place for sound. It had been her mother's studio, Marta's favorite place in the world. Memories were in every corner of every room there, and until now, Lucky had been unwilling—or unable—to face them.

But she wasn't going to question his motives, not when those motives had brought her the man of her dreams.

LUCKY SAT in the darkened library later that afternoon, nursing a Scotch and wondering where he'd gone wrong. He never drank this early in the day, but this was an exception.

As a senior-grade PAX operative, he solved problems for a living; the bigger and more potentially lethal the problem, the better he liked it. Renegade spies. Hijacked nuclear weapons. Assassination plots that could rock the country to her core.

But this problem had him hog-tied.

"You're a damn fool," he muttered, pouring himself another Scotch from the decanter on the side table. Another man would have seen it coming and made sure the two of them never got within a country mile of each other.

But not Lucky Wilde. He knew his daughters, and he'd been sure he didn't have a thing to worry about. Trask was too poor for Sam and he was too old for Frankie. And Martie—hell, all Martie cared about was squirreling herself away in that attic workroom of hers, morning, noon and night.

No, he'd been so sure they wouldn't give his young protégé a second glance that he'd gotten careless, letting the two distinct halves of his life come together the way he'd sworn he'd never do again.

He let the Scotch burn its way down his throat and into his belly. The glow on Martie's face lingered in his mind, making him think of things he hadn't thought about in years. Love was an unruly emotion. It didn't follow any logical pattern or play by anyone's rules. And sometimes believing you were in love could be every bit as powerful as the real thing itself.

Trask denied there was anything going on and, for the moment, Lucky believed him. But what those two young people were feeling couldn't be satisfied for long by sunrise drives and longing looks. Sooner or later they would want more, need more, until they were in so far there could be no turning back.

He's not the one for you, darlin'. His Martie needed someone who'd be around for the long haul, and he knew Trask Benedict wasn't that kind.

The boy seethed with rage, a bone-deep anger that made him perfect for Lucky's purposes, but one hell of a bad bet for his daughter.

Fatigue washed over him like a summer breeze. His years in the shadows had taken their toll. You couldn't see the ugliness he'd seen and not be affected by it.

Maybe he wasn't doing the boy such a favor, taking him under his wing. Maybe he would have helped him more by letting him find his own way. But there had been something about the boy that touched Lucky. *You see yourself in him, old man.* The mistakes, the dreams, the love he'd searched long and hard to find, only to lose it in the most terrible way.

Too late, he thought, finishing the Scotch. There was no point in second-guessing himself now. The great machinery of the PAX organization was in motion, and in less than three weeks Trask would vanish into it, leaving Martie behind.

If Lucky had his way, it couldn't happen soon enough.

THEY MET whenever they could that first week, stolen moments carved from the day like sparkling gemstones from solid rock.

Ten minutes alone in the gazebo while a spring storm created a curtain of rain to shield them from the world.

A picnic supper while Lucky was up in Dallas on business.

Touching. Kissing. Wanting.

Dear God, how they wanted...

It was all new to Trask, new and vibrant and so *right* that he felt as if he'd been handed the keys to the life he'd always wanted but never believed he could have.

Somehow, in the blink of an eye, she'd become part of him, heart and soul. He'd been with other women in the past, known the heat and hunger of desire, but nothing like this. The day after they met, she'd given him a silver ring she'd made, with one of those blue stones he'd admired set in the middle of the unpolished metal. "To ease your heart," she'd said, then kissed him, and he'd understood.

She was the first thing he thought of in the morning when he opened his eyes. She was with him during the day as he worked in the guest cottage. Her lovely face was in his dreams at night.

Yesterday, he'd pulled her into the shadows of the live oak trees that divided the property and kissed her with all the rage and passion and loneliness bottled up inside him, and it hadn't been enough. Not even close to enough.

Her eyes had widened as he pulled her against his body, letting her feel how much he wanted her. She'd drawn away, trying to put space between herself and his intensity, but he'd only held her tighter. He'd found himself wanting to tell her the whole story—but PAX meant too much to him and, in a way, so did Lucky Wilde.

They'd told him that real life would be the hardest test of all, and they hadn't been kidding. This whole charade about installing a sound system in the guest house was harder to maintain than slipping into a hostile nation and getting out with the crown jewels.

"Trask!"

He spun around to find Martie standing in the doorway of the guest house. Her dark hair was piled on top of her head, and she wore a short cotton dress the same aqua color as her eyes.

"What are you doing here?" he asked, shoving some documents beneath the love seat, then rising to his feet. "I thought I was off-limits when Lucky was home."

Her lush mouth curved in a smile. "You are off-limits."

Heat gathered low in his belly. "We still on for later?" An hour near the pond, away from prying eyes. It wasn't much, and it was everything.

Her eyes seemed to darken from aqua to deep turquoise as she looked at him. "No," she said. "We're not still on for later." She stepped into the room and closed the door behind her. "You don't mind, do you?"

"No," he said, as the heat turned into a raging fire. "Not one damn bit."

"Good," she said softly. "That's what I hoped you'd say."

MARTIE'S RELIEF was so intense that her knees went weak. She'd never done anything like this before, never even imagined being so bold, but she loved him so much that she would move mountains if it meant they could be together.

She watched as the muscles of his left cheek clenched then unclenched. "Do you know what you're doing, Martie?"

She nodded as her heart beat wildly inside her chest. "I've always known." She'd known from the first moment she saw him that it would lead to this.

"Your father?"

"Chicago," she said, as laughter bubbled up inside her. "Until tomorrow night." Her sisters had gone with him.

"We're alone?"

"Except for the help."

One moment they were standing on opposite sides of the room, and the next they were wrapped in each other's arms. Everything she'd ever done, every breath she'd ever drawn—now it all made sense.

He swept her up in his arms, and she rested her hot cheek against his chest. His heart beat heavily beneath her ear, the fast drumming of his blood echoed by the beat of her own heart. This was right, she thought, as he carried her toward the bed-room. Everything about it was right.

He laid her down gently on the narrow bed, against the pillows with their soft white covers that smelled of him. She felt dizzy, as if the world were turning faster and faster and the only thing that kept her from spinning off into the galaxy was the man who lay beside her.

No one had ever looked at him that way before, with such innocent hunger. It was almost his un-doing. Didn't she know that sex was about need and heat, and that love had nothing to do with it?

He understood the powerful drive to lose your-self in a woman's warmth, to use her softness to ease the hard edges of your soul. But that had ev-erything to do with lust, and damn little to do with love.

Now he wasn't so sure. She made him feel things, this wide-eyed girl did, things that were so far be-yond his experience that he wondered if in some way this was his first time, too. He didn't have to ask her to know she had never been in a man's bed before. It was there in every movement she made, the sweet trembling of her breath against his mouth as he claimed her with a kiss.

She moved restlessly beneath him, her hands tracing small patterns along his spine.

"I want you naked." His words made her shiver with delight.

"That's how I want you," she whispered, filled with a sense of power she'd never known she possessed. She wanted to feel his body against hers, skin to skin, heat to heat.

Slowly he undid the buttons at the front of her dress. His fingers brushed against the swell of her breasts, and her breath caught in her throat. He slid the straps of her plain white bra off her shoulders, then lowered his head until she felt his silky dark hair brush her skin.

Instinctively she cupped the back of his head, drawing him closer, in a gesture that was more womanly than she realized.

She moaned softly as he freed her breasts, and Trask thought he would go up in flames from wanting her. She was so small, so perfect, her breasts more beautiful than he'd dared to imagine. He drew her nipple into his mouth and suckled, and her back arched as she offered herself up to him more completely.

She couldn't think, couldn't breathe. When he released her nipple, she felt bereft. When he drew her other nipple into the warm, wet cavern of his mouth, she felt as if she'd spun out into the universe and touched the sun.

And she wanted more. She wanted to belong to him in the most basic way possible, to open for him and be claimed by him.

To own him.

He pulled the shirt over his head and threw it across the room. Light sparkled against the silver ring she'd made for him. He was lean, hard, beautifully muscled. A fine hunger built inside her belly as she tensed, waiting. His eyes were dark as he looked at her, and she began to tremble, with both anticipation and fear.

He unfastened the last buttons on her dress, then slipped it down over her arms, letting it slide off the bed, where it lay on the cool tile floor in a soft aqua heap. He unhooked the front clasp on her bra. It quickly joined her dress.

She lay across the yellow quilt, naked except for the scrap of white lace that covered her mound. He wanted to rip away the lace with his teeth, but knew she wasn't ready for that. Not yet. Instead, he reached for the snap on his jeans. The rasp of the zipper seemed to echo in the quiet room. His briefs did nothing to hide his powerful erection. He stripped them off, as well. Her cheeks reddened, and she glanced away.

"You can look," he said, lying next to her. "I don't mind."

He was teasing her, but she didn't laugh. She couldn't. She scooted to the other edge of the bed. "I don't think I want to do this anymore."

"I think you do." His voice was low, seductive, infinitely persuasive.

"I—" She gestured toward him. "How?"

He gathered her close to him, covering her with his body. Her breasts flattened against his chest. The thick mat of hair tickled her skin. There was something intoxicating about skin against skin, something that made her feel as if her blood had somehow turned to champagne in her veins. She ran her hands along the tight muscles of his shoulders, down the length of his spine, then curved over the swell of his buttocks.

His erection burned against the tops of her thighs. She gasped as he brought a hand between the two of them and cupped her against his palm.

"You're wet," he murmured against her lips. "Wet and hot."

Her mind exploded. His words were a powerful aphrodisiac. Her thighs parted, and she arched her back. She felt empty...hungry...impatient....

She bit at the spot where his shoulder met his neck.

That swift arrow of pain sharpened his pleasure. He slid one finger into her. She was small and tight, silken muscles rippling in anticipation.

A dark fire was spreading throughout her body, a coiling, dangerous fire that only he could ease. Time and again he brought her to the brink with his hand and his mouth, until she found herself on the edge of anger and need.

"Do you want this?" His voice was husky, rough, as he brought her hand to rest against his erection.

"Yes," she said, the word a dark whisper. "Yes!"

Chapter Four

The pain was swift and sharp as the delicate barrier gave way to his demands, and she cried out. For a moment, she wanted to push him off her, to change her mind, but then the pain gave way to something so amazing, so overpowering, that she was helpless before the onslaught. A willing captive.

As she lay beneath him, her eyes welled with tears, and he gentled her with words and kisses while he fought to control his own surging desire.

But he was only human, and she made him feel powerful and protective and so hungry for her that he almost lost the battle before it began. He wanted to show her how it could be between a man and a woman when it was right. He didn't want her to remember their first time—*her* first time—as anything but the miracle it was.

Because this was a miracle.

In a world that didn't offer much in the way of miracles, he'd found one, and he wasn't about to let her go.

That narrow bed by the window became the center of his world, and she the center of his universe.

Afternoon turned to evening, and still they lay together, sometimes making love, sometimes simply rejoicing in the amazing fact that they'd found each other.

"We're so lucky," she whispered to him as the vibrant colors of a Texas sunset washed across the bed. "Some people go their whole lives and never find someone to love."

Her words found their mark inside his heart. He'd been alone for so long. Hell, he'd believed he would be alone for the rest of his life. Nothing he'd ever seen or heard had made him believe any different . . . until now. She had changed everything.

It was the same for Martie. She felt as if she'd been wandering through the darkness alone until he came into her life and handed her the sun and moon and stars. All the puzzle pieces had suddenly fallen into place, pieces she hadn't even realized were missing. She knew now where she was going and how to get there and, most important of all, she knew that the two of them would be together forever.

"NOT MUCH LONGER, Mr. Wilde." The flight attendant gathered up Lucky's coffee cup and newspapers in preparation for landing. "Maybe another fifteen minutes until we're on the ground."

Lucky bit back his irritation. "What about the car?"

The attendant's smile widened. "It'll be waiting for you, just like you requested."

He nodded. As a rule, he engaged his employees in conversation. The bits and pieces of their lives were important to him, and they knew it. Today, however, he had other things on his mind.

He damned the foul weather that had delayed him in Caracas an extra day. Something was going on back home in Houston, something that could destroy a pair of young lives before they even had a chance, and he needed to stop it before it went too far.

"Damnation," he muttered, peering out the window at the predawn sky. *If it hadn't gone too far already.*

He was fifty-five years old. He had seen much of what life had to offer... and felt the sharp sting of fate's vengeance when he buried two wives before their time. He'd ruled his life by a combination of instinct and logic, and both had served him well.

Lucky wasn't a superstitious man, but the feeling of impending doom that had settled on him the night of his Martie's birthday was too strong now to be denied.

The seat belt sign flickered on overhead, and he gave a reflexive tug. He shouldn't have left them alone together. What in hell had he been thinking of? That was like storing dynamite in a room filled with matches—or ignoring the sparks between Martie and Trask.

Only a damn fool would be surprised by the explosion.

He reminds you of yourself, old man....

That hunger for life. The need to test his own limits. The boy had grown up with money, and he had position if he wanted it, but something else drove him, something dark and angry that could only be conquered by confronting his demons.

Lucky understood that. He knew all about conquering demons, and how sometimes those very demons could lead a man to discover all that was good and strong about himself, and he prayed that would happen for Trask.

Would he ever forget the expression in Martie's eyes when she looked at Trask? She was his middle child, the one who didn't share his blood but owned his heart, yet there was a part of his beloved daughter that he'd never been able to reach. A bone-deep loneliness that not even the love of her family could erase.

But that boy could. He'd seen it in her eyes when she looked at him. The open, vulnerable expression of a girl on the verge of womanhood. A girl falling in love for the first time.

"Damnation," he muttered as the private jet touched down. Why did she have to fall in love with the one man she couldn't have? The one who was guaranteed to break her heart?

Today, he thought as he gathered up his papers and folded his glasses back into their case. Today he would tell the boy it was time to go.

THE SOUND of gravel crunching in the driveway woke Martie up with a start. She leaned up on one elbow and peered through the curtained window.

"Oh, my God!" Naked, she leapt from bed and made a frenzied attempt at gathering up her clothes.

Trask mumbled something in his sleep and rolled over.

"Wake up!" Her voice was shrill. "Trask, Daddy's home!"

He yawned, then patted the empty spot next to him. "Come back to bed."

"Are you insane?" she shrieked. "He's going to kill me!"

"We haven't done anything wrong, Martie," he said, in a voice still husky from sleep.

She glared at him, struggling into her panties and bra while she tried to keep from hyperventilating. "Try explaining that to Daddy when he's pointing a gun at you."

Trask laughed, in a rolling baritone that made her toes curl despite the situation. "Come here."

She snatched her dress from the floor. "You must be crazy."

"He's going to find out about us anyway. Might as well be now."

She slipped the dress over her head, then tugged it into place. "You're definitely crazy," she said, shuddering. "I don't think there's a father on earth who wants to hear that his daughter—" Her cheeks flamed at the thought.

"That his daughter was going to be married."

She leapt onto the bed and threw herself into his arms, joy exploding inside her chest like fireworks on the Fourth of July.

Lucky might be upset that his seventeen-year-old daughter had found the man she intended to marry, but he would get over it once he realized how much she and Trask loved each other.

She would love to have her father's blessing, but even if he withheld it, that didn't change things. Nothing would keep her and Trask apart.

Nothing.

"No." Trask leaned across the big oak desk and met Lucky's eyes. "Not now."

Lucky leaned back in his chair and propped his feet up on the blotter. "Afraid you don't have much choice in this, boy. The plane's waiting for you at the airport."

The old man looked too casual. Too matter-of-fact. Trask's adrenaline level went up two notches. "We need to talk," he said, meeting Lucky's eyes.

"No time. The car's outside. Go pack your gear and get rolling."

"You don't understand," Trask began. "I—"

"No!" Lucky roared. "*You* don't understand! When you signed on with the organization, you gave up your right to say when and where you want to be. You belong to them now, boy."

Trask could barely hear over the fierce pounding of his blood. He'd sworn to Martie that nothing would tear him away from her, and he meant it. Damn PAX, and anything else that tried to come between them.

He leveled his gaze on Lucky. "I love your daughter."

The old man flinched as if Trask had struck him a blow. "You've only known her a week."

"Ten days."

"You can't fall in love in ten days."

"You're wrong," Trask said quietly. "I fell in love with her the minute I saw her."

Lucky glanced toward the window. A bead of sweat trickled down Trask's back. He hadn't expected the old man to jump for joy at the idea that his little girl wasn't a little girl any longer, but this was something other than paternal concern.

Anger would have been better. Hell, a left to the jaw would have been better. Anything but this long-drawn-out silence.

"So what is it, Lucky? I'm not good enough for your daughter?"

Lucky met his eyes head-on. "That's part of it."

Trask's laugh was bitter. "If it's money you're worried about, my trust fund's bigger than hers, and you know it."

"I don't give a damn about your money," Lucky snapped. "It's my daughter I'm worried about."

"I'm not going to hurt her."

"You can't know that."

"The hell I can't."

"There are things you don't understand, things you don't know anything about."

"Right," said Trask. "And there are things you're too damn old to remember."

"You're wrong, boy. I remember all of it."

"Then you know how we feel, Lucky. We're going to be together whether you like it or not, so why don't you give us your blessings now and get it over with?"

"What about PAX?"

"What about them?" Trask countered.

"You've made a commitment."

"So did you. That didn't stop you from having a wife and family."

"You don't know what you're talking about, boy. There's a whole hell of a lot you don't know."

"There's nothing you can tell me that's going to change my mind about Martie."

"You say you love her."

"Yes," Trask said, "I—"

Lucky raised his hand, cutting off Trask's words. "How much do you love her?"

This was it, the big question. All he had to do was answer it honestly, from the heart, and there was nothing more Lucky could say.

"I'm waitin', boy."

He drew in a deep breath, then met the old man's eyes head-on. "I'd give my life for her."

He waited for Lucky to say something, but his words were met with silence. The old man should be jumping for joy.

He forced a cocky grin. "I'll pass on the dowry, Lucky. You might even be able to convince me to kick in on the wedding."

"Sit down," Lucky said.

"Hey, it's over, isn't it? I passed your test, now I can—"

"For the love of God, sit down and listen."

Trask felt the way he had when his parents' attorney told him about their death—cold and clammy and desperate to deny the truth of what was happening.

IT WOULD TAKE a tougher man than Lucky Wilde had ever claimed to be to turn his back on what Trask and Martie felt for each other, but he had no choice. He couldn't take the risk. He'd done his best to shield his children from the danger he knew was out there, and he'd been successful. If Martie married Trask, she would be in greater peril than Lucky could fight.

"Sit down," Lucky said again, his voice gentled this time by emotion, "and listen to me."

"I don't want to hear it." The boy's eyes were shadowed with fear. He looked young, vulnerable beneath the cocky facade. Lucky hated being the one to end his dreams.

But the boy had to hear it. And Lucky had to be the one to tell him. Neither one of them had a choice in it anymore, not when Martie's life hung in the balance.

You would've been real good for her, son, he thought as the weight of this sorry world pressed against his chest. *But I don't want to lose my little girl the same way I lost her mama.*

WHAT ON EARTH was taking them so long?

Martie had been waiting on the landing for over

an hour, and still there was no sign of Trask or her father. Everyone knew Lucky was the most stubborn man in Texas, but even Lucky couldn't possibly take this long to see reason.

She leaned over the banister, tilting her head in the direction of her father's study. Nothing. Not one single sound. What were they doing, speaking in sign language? She'd expected to hear a loud roar of disapproval, followed by a full dose of male bluster. The one thing she hadn't expected was silence.

Silence made her edgy. The big house always rocked with sound. Lucky's booming laughter. The whine of central air-conditioning. Rock music from Frankie's room, and soft classical from Sam's. It was never quiet, not even in the dead of night.

But it was quiet now, and she knew that wasn't a good sign.

"That does it," she said out loud. The sound of her voice calmed her. No more standing here on the landing, waiting while Trask and Lucky discussed her future. She'd been charmed that Trask wanted to ask formally for her hand in marriage, but it was taking entirely too long.

She hurried down the stairs, then raced toward her father's study. This was her life. Trask was the man she loved and wanted to spend the rest of her days with, and she wasn't going to cower in the shadows like some stupid little wimp.

She was a few feet away from Lucky's study when she heard a car engine start up in the driveway. Every muscle in her body stiffened, and for a moment she stood perfectly still, as a sense of dread replaced the elation that had bubbled through her veins a second ago. *How stupid,* she thought. Cars came and went all day long at the house. There was nothing to get so upset about.

The study door was slightly ajar. "Trask?" she called, pushing it open the rest of the day. "Daddy?"

The room was empty. Lucky's brown leather desk chair was shoved up against the window wall. A pewter mug lay upturned on the polished oak floor, with sharpened number-two pencils scattered all around it. The faint aroma of Lucky's favorite cigars lingered in the air, but the stink of anger overpowered it.

She jumped at the sound of another car engine starting up. Pulling back the curtains, she peered out the window in time to see her father steering his favorite Caddy down the driveway. Maybe Trask was in the guest cottage.

But he wasn't. She searched the cottage, the main house and the property, but he was nowhere to be found. The housekeeper hadn't seen him since last night. Neither had any of the kitchen help, the gardener or the pool man. It was as if he'd vanished into thin air.

"Idiot," she muttered, pacing up and down the length of the driveway. For all she knew, Trask hadn't even had a chance to tell her father that they wanted to be married. Lucky had probably sent Trask out to run an errand, then gone off to the store himself.

Later, she told herself as she went back into the house. She'd shower, eat a late breakfast, and then, before she knew it, Trask would be back and she could find out what had happened between him and Lucky.

THE WILDES' HOUSEKEEPER, Carlota, appeared in the doorway to the sun-room a little before six o'clock. "Will your daddy be home for dinner, Miss Martie?"

Martie turned away from the window. "I was hoping you'd know the answer to that, Carlota."

"Nobody tells me anything," Carlota griped. "Don't know whether Angela should set the table for one or two or an army."

"Set it for three," she said firmly, then turned back to the window.

An hour passed.

And then another.

Carlota complained that the roast chicken was turning to rubber in the kitchen. Martie told her not to worry, that she'd be just as happy with sandwiches whenever Trask and Lucky got home.

Finally, a few minutes before midnight, Lucky walked slowly into the sun-room.

"Where have you *been*?" Martie demanded as she took in her father's disheveled appearance. "Where's Trask?"

Lucky headed for the bar and poured himself a little bourbon and branch. "Don't suppose there's any dinner left for your old daddy, is there?"

She ignored his question. "Where's Trask, Daddy?" she asked, her voice rising in agitation. "Have you fired him? He needs this job! If you've fired him, I'll never—"

Her father raised his hand. "The boy's gone, darlin'."

"I can't believe you did it!" She threw her hands in the air in disgust. "You fired him because of me, didn't you?"

"Darlin', listen—"

"I don't want to listen." She began to pace the room. "Where is he? Call him right now and tell him you made a mistake."

"I can't do that," Lucky said quietly.

"Of course you can do that," she snapped. "He didn't just disappear into the mist. You must have a phone number for him. Call and—"

"Sit down, darlin'."

"No!" She quickened her pace, trying to keep one step ahead of the terrible look in her father's eyes. "I had to grow up sometime, Daddy. I thought you knew that."

He put down his tumbler of bourbon and branch and walked toward her.

"Oh, God," she said, moving toward the door. "I don't want to hear this, Daddy. Please don't—"

"Trask is gone, darlin', and he isn't coming back."

"That's not true! He loves me. He wants to marry me. He'd never leave without me."

Lucky placed his hands on her shoulders. "Sit down," he said.

Her knees were trembling so badly that she listened to him and took a seat on the rattan bench near the French doors.

"You did something, didn't you, Daddy?" she whispered. Something terrible, something a man without money or position was powerless to fight.

"The boy asked for your hand, darlin', and I refused."

Her temper flared. "That won't stop us. We wanted your blessing, but we don't need it. We'll get married whether you like it or not."

"We had words," Lucky went on, ignoring her outburst. "He had himself all riled up when he stormed out of here."

A loud buzzing began inside her head, and her hands started to tremble. *I don't want to hear this. Please don't make me hear this....*

"He jumped into my old Chevy and roared out of here."

"He'll drive around until he cools off, and then he'll come back and we can talk about our engagement."

"No, Martie," her father said, in a voice heavy with sorrow. "He's not coming back."

"You don't know that! I know him better than anyone in the world. He'll be back for me."

Her father crouched down in front of her and gathered her shaking hands between his. "I don't want to say this, darlin'—"

"Then don't!" A hysterical laugh tore from her throat. "Don't say it ... don't say it ..."

"There was an accident ..."

"Please, Daddy—"

"... out past the airport ..."

"I don't want to hear this.... Please, I don't—"

"He's gone, darlin'. I'm sorry, but the boy is dead."

"You're lying," she said, even though she knew her father had never told her anything but the truth. "You'd say anything to keep us apart."

Lucky looked anguished, as if the weight of the world and all of its problems had settled on his shoulders, and she knew that her dreams would never come true.

"It's true," she whispered. "Oh, God, it's true."

Something ugly and dark ripped at her heart and, lowering her head, she began to cry.

NOW

It is only with the heart that one can see rightly;
what is essential is invisible to the eye.

—Antoine de Saint-Exupéry

Chapter Five

Martie Wilde was halfway to the country club when she noticed the enormous run laddering its way up her leg.

An omen, she thought. Even her panty hose thought she was making a mistake.

She leaned forward and tapped Hank, her dad's limo driver, on the shoulder. "Hank, would you do me a favor and pull into Fiesta? I have to buy a pair of stockings, or they'll think I can't dress myself."

"You're runnin' real late, Martie," Hank said as he stopped the car near the door. "You better hustle, if you don't want your party to start without you."

"They wouldn't dare start the party without me," she said. "I'm the happy bride-to-be, aren't I?"

The truth was, the happy bride-to-be had been engrossed in a spectacular jewelry design for a member of the British royal family and had completely forgotten about the party.

Another omen.

"Wait right here," she said, leaping from the car before it rolled to a complete stop. "I won't be a minute."

"You sure you don't want me to come in with you? You're wearin' some real pretty baubles. Hate to see you took hostage by the frozen foods."

Hank laughed at his joke, and she joined in, although the underlying truth of his words didn't escape either one of them. A funny sense of apprehension made her scalp tingle, but she dismissed it as the beginning of a sinus headache. What could happen in a supermarket?

She hurried inside, dashed up the aisle where they kept sweat socks, T-shirts and stockings, and quickly found what she needed.

Which was how she came to be standing on the express checkout line, clutching a plastic egg in one hand and a five-dollar bill in the other, when she turned and saw him and remembered why it was that men and women had been created different.

It hit her like a thunderbolt, an unexpected, overwhelming sense of destiny that she'd experienced once before, and never again—until now.

Quit staring at him, Martie. Engaged women aren't supposed to ogle strange men.

As a rule, she didn't even ogle men she knew. Since that long-ago springtime, the romantic side of her nature had only been given sway in her work.

This, however, was different. She had no control over it. She couldn't have turned away from him at that moment if someone had dropped a bomb on the express checkout line.

He was leaning against the ATM, arms folded across his chest, watching her the way other men of her acquaintance watched the Oilers play football. It had been a long time since she'd had a man's undivided attention, and she wasn't exactly sure what to do with it.

Her younger sister, Frankie, would have blown the guy a kiss.

Her older sister, Sam, a reformed flirt, would have called the cops and claimed sexual harassment.

All Martie could do was stare at him.

He was tall and dark, but he wasn't handsome. His face was too rough, his features were too battered. The face of a man who'd lived a life she couldn't imagine.

Handsome? No. But *dangerous* came close, and *lethal weapon* was even better. He topped six feet by an inch or two, and had the kind of lean, sinewy build that she'd always found particularly devastating.

Not that she had any right to be devastated.

She was, after all, engaged to be married to a man she didn't love and who didn't love her in return. It wasn't a perfect situation, not by a long shot, but it would never break her heart, and that was enough for her.

"Ma'am."

She blinked. The cashier was waving to her.

"It's your turn, ma'am."

Behind her, an elderly woman muttered something, then nudged her with the nose of her shopping cart, which, under normal circumstances, would have made Martie crazy. This time she ignored it. She had more important things to think about.

Like whether or not she remembered how to breathe.

A slight smile tilted the left corner of his wide and sensual mouth, punctuated by a wicked scar that curved along his cheekbone. Swift and unbidden, a sense memory washed over her as she remembered a mouth that had claimed hers back when she still believed in happy endings.

Over the years, she'd mastered the art of not thinking about him, of pretending her heart hadn't died right along with him, so it came as a surprise that today, of all days, it would all come rushing back.

She didn't want to remember him. She'd given him her innocence and he'd given her his love, and it had all ended on a stretch of highway near the airport. She'd managed to burn away the memory of his voice, his smell, his touch, and one day she'd even manage to burn away the memory of how it had felt to be loved so deeply and so well that you thought you would die of it.

Strange that this angry-looking man would bring it all back to her. He looked nothing like Trask Benedict. From his chiseled cheekbones to his sculptured jaw, Trask had been blessed with the face of an angel.

This man hadn't been so lucky. His features were irregular, his skin was weathered and marred by scars. He wore faded jeans and a white T-shirt. The faint glimmer of a plain silver chain showed around his neck. He looked like he'd spent most of his time straddling a motorcycle in search of adventures she'd rather not consider. And not just any motorcycle, she thought. A Harley. One of those massive machines that screamed sex at seventy miles per hour.

You've lost your mind, Martie. Since when do you think this way?

He was still watching her. A smarter woman would probably be offended by the intensity of his gaze, but it thrilled her, even if she was reasonably certain it was her dress and not her that had grabbed his attention. You didn't see too many bright blue beaded cocktail dresses in the supermarket these days, not even in Texas.

His gaze unsettled her, yet there was something oddly familiar about it, something intimate, which was absolutely ridiculous, considering the fact she'd never seen this man before in her life.

She knew what she should do. After all, she was on her way to her own engagement party. Any decent, upstanding almost-married woman would shoot him a withering glance and turn away in a self-righteous huff.

Still, he was flirting with her, or at least she thought he was, even if his expression hadn't changed by a millimeter. He was staring into her eyes as if they were lovers, as if they shared a secret from the world.

I wish—

She caught herself. Fantasies like that were dangerous. Better to confine her romantic reveries to her choice of reading material and her jewelry designs.

But would it be so terrible if she flirted with him? The idea sent a thrill of excitement rippling through her. She'd never once flirted with her fiancé, Jason Blackburn. The thought had never even occurred to her.

This is your last chance, Martie. Might as well give it your best shot.

Her lips curved in a tentative smile.

His brows knotted in a scowl.

She wished the linoleum would open up and swallow her whole.

"That'll be three dollars, seventeen cents," said the cashier.

Martie turned away from the man standing by the ATM and handed the clerk her five-dollar bill. The clerk popped the plastic egg into a plastic bag, then handed it to Martie, along with her change. The transaction took maybe fifteen seconds.

Which was just long enough for the mystery man to disappear.

DYING WAS EASY.

Seeing her again was hard.

How many times had he run through the scene in his mind, tried to imagine how it would feel to see her lovely face again, hear the sound of her voice? Still, nothing had prepared him for the reality.

He folded himself behind a towering display of canned corn, tomato soup and pinto beans, and cursed his bad timing. The ATM had been about to cough up a few hundred dollars that didn't belong to him when he saw her standing there on line in her glittery blue dress and fancy jewelry, looking like a displaced princess on leave from the palace.

What in hell were the odds of bumping into her at Fiesta? He'd been hanging around the cash machine, waiting for his chance to pounce on a forgotten card, when he turned around and *bam!* He was twenty-four again, and in love for the first and only time in his life.

It wasn't like he hadn't expected to see her tonight. You didn't plan on crashing a woman's engagement party without expecting to bump into her over the cheese dip. He'd told himself that she was part of the past, that what they'd had didn't matter any longer, and maybe he'd even believed it for a little while, but the moment he looked into her aqua eyes he'd seen the past ten years for the lie they were.

He could've handled it at the party. Big crowds were sterile. Anonymous. People checked their emotions at the door when they went to those things, and he would've been no exception. That was easy for him. Or at least it had been before he met her.

He supposed he should be glad she hadn't recognized him. Hell, he didn't recognize himself when he looked into the mirror. Coming back from the dead had changed him inside, while his captors had taken care of everything else. The only things he had in common with the man she'd loved were height, weight and shoe size.

For the past two weeks he'd been trying every way he could think of to get to Lucky, but with no success. The engagement party was his last chance. Lucky was the only person on earth who would believe the fantastic and terrifying story he had to tell—and understand the danger this placed him in.

Phase one of the plan to gain control of the world was ready to be put into operation, and once it got rolling, it would take a miracle to stop it.

A sharp pain under his third rib, left side, reminded him that they were closing in. Among other things, the microchip served as an electronic tracking device. Trask could only hope they were still too far away to get a precise take on his whereabouts. Once PAX had lauded that microchip as the beginning of a new age of communication; now it was the foundation of impending disaster.

Trask had been on the run since January, going from continent to continent, country to country, trying to find someone who would believe him. Doors that had been open to him were closed now. He had a new face and a different voice. His retinal pattern had been altered and his fingerprints eliminated. He couldn't access his bank accounts, talk to old friends, breach even the lowest level of PAX security in order to be heard.

He knew the story sounded like something from a Steven Spielberg movie, the kind of over-the-top fiction that should be packaged with a bucket of popcorn and a large Coke. But it was true and it was happening to him and if someone didn't believe him, and soon, the world as they knew it would be a thing of the past.

He watched as Martie strolled casually past the ATM, then took a quick right near the produce aisle. He crouched lower behind the canned corn. It was hard to be inconspicuous when you were six feet three inches tall, but he'd give it his best shot.

The years had been good to her. Her dark hair was clipped short now, a silky bob that barely reached her chin. It was all angles and gloss, a hell of a lot more sophisticated than he would have expected. Still, it worked. She carried herself differently now, but he supposed that came with the territory. She wasn't a naive young girl any longer, she was a woman.

A woman about to be married.

"Mommy!" A child's voice sounded to his right. "Look at the man!"

A brown-haired kid about the size of a large terrier peered at him from around the display.

The ache beneath his rib cage turned into a sharply burning pain.

A brown-haired woman pushing a shopping cart joined the kid. "Oh!" She stared down at Trask, eyes wide. Now he knew how animals in a zoo felt. "Do you need help?"

"No." This was no time to be polite.

"You're sitting down." The kid was obviously a budding brain surgeon. "Did you fall?"

He ignored the question. Kids were a lot like cats: Encourage them and they'd never go away.

The mother sized up the situation quickly. Decent, upstanding citizens didn't lurk behind displays of canned vegetables. "Come on, honey," she said, placing a protective hand on the kid's shoulder. "Let's find your sister."

She handled that shopping cart the way some men he knew handled automatic weapons. You had to admire a woman like that.

The kid lingered, staring openly at the scar on Trask's cheek. "That's ugly," he said. "How'd you get it?"

"Your mother's calling, kid."

"Wish I had a scar," the kid said. "It looks cool. My mom won't even let me get a stick-on tattoo."

"Get lost," Trask growled. Short of growing fangs, it was the best he could do.

Apparently it was good enough. The kid's eyes widened. He took a step backward, then another, straight into the the sharp metal edge of the display shelf. Too shocked to cry out, he fell forward at Trask's feet. Blood was spreading across the back of his torn Power Rangers T-shirt. Trask had seen wounds like that before—ugly, jagged tears that left a nasty scar and sometimes even worse. He knew all about nasty scars, and he wouldn't wish them on a kid.

He hated the process. It hurt like hell at the best of times, and now it was fraught with real danger as well. It was a risky thing to do, but the microchip embedded beneath his left third rib had been silent for a while, and pain was only one way of reminding yourself you were alive.

And even if he didn't like to admit it, maybe he still had just enough humanity to want to help a kid.

"You're okay," he said in a low voice, as he turned the child onto his side. "You're not hurt."

The kid's face was ashen, and his lips were dry. Trask saw the disbelief. He didn't blame him. The kid's small body was racked with pain and the more it hurt, the more terrified he got, and here was this guy telling him he wasn't hurt at all.

"Trust me, kid," he said, placing his hands on the kid's narrow back. "This is gonna hurt me a lot more than it hurts you."

It did. The pain staggered Trask, nearly knocking him to the ground, but he could take it. As long as they were too far away to activate the reverse process, everything would be all right.

Great screaming waves of agony ripped up his spine and tore at his gut. He absorbed the kid's pain, and with it his own fear. Moments later, it was all over.

He rocked back on his heels, exhausted. The tear in the kid's shirt had vanished. So had the wound. The kid stared at him, his brown eyes round with wonder.

"See?" Trask grinned at him. "Told you you were okay."

The kid's mother popped up at the far end of the aisle. "David Samuel Collins, if you're not right here next to me by the time I count to three, no Power Rangers for a month."

"But, Ma—"

"One . . ."

"Better go," said Trask. "You can't miss Power Rangers."

"But—"

"Two . . ."

The kid was obviously torn.

"What's the big deal?" Trask said with a nonchalant shrug of his shoulders. "You fell. I picked you up. Nothing to miss your favorite show over, is it?"

The kid knew better, but when you were eight years old, the boundaries between the possible and the fantastic were blurred, and things like Power Rangers and a mother's wrath carry more weight than a minor miracle.

Nice to know that in a world bent on destroying everything good and right and decent, some things never changed.

"MISSION ACCOMPLISHED," Martie said as she climbed back into the limousine. She'd change her hose in the ladies' room when she reached the country club.

"You okay?" Hank asked, swiveling around in his seat to look at her. "Your face is real red."

"I ran to the car," she said. "Guess I'm not in very good shape."

Hank narrowed his eyes and took a good long look at her. "That ain't it."

She felt her cheeks grow even hotter. "I can't imagine what else it could be, Hank." *Oh, yes, you can, Martie.*

"You look like you seen a ghost."

"No ghosts," she said with a laugh. "Not a single one."

Just a man who'd made her remember the way it was supposed to be.

Chapter Six

"Martie." Jason's voice pierced her gloom two hours later. He sounded annoyed, which only fueled her bad mood. "My mother was complimenting the vegetable terrine."

You compliment the chef, Jason, she thought sourly. *You don't compliment the asparagus.*

She looked across the magnificent cherrywood table, around the centerpiece of yellow roses and freesia, and met the eyes of the man she had agreed to spend the rest of her natural-born life with.

They were squinty little eyes, like two pieces of flint slapped into the middle of his face. She'd known Jason for years. Why had it taken her so long to notice he had squinty eyes? She tried to imagine seeing those eyes peering from her across a pillow but the thought made her shudder.

"Thank you, Margaret," she said, accepting the compliment on behalf of vegetables everywhere. "The club is known for its cuisine."

And for the fact that it had been the first to open its doors to minorities, something Margaret Blackburn wouldn't care to hear. Margaret believed in equal opportunity, as long as *their* opportunities were at least three towns away from *her* opportunities.

"I'm so distressed that your dear father isn't here," Margaret was saying. "It simply isn't the same without him."

Margaret's most innocuous comments somehow managed to carry a venomous sting. It was one of her more endearing traits.

"I'm sure we all feel the same way," Martie said smoothly. She hadn't suffered through two summers of Miss Adelaide's School of Deportment for nothing. She could lie with the best of them. "I told Daddy we could postpone the party until he's feeling more like his old self, but he insisted we go ahead with things as planned."

Margaret Blackburn dabbed at her eyes with a lace-trimmed hankie she kept in her purse for such occasions. "How like Lucky to be so considerate."

Martie stood up, a bland smile fixed firmly on her face. "Jason, you make sure Margaret's glass is filled. I'll be right back."

She fled for the ladies' room as if the hounds of hell were nipping at the heels of her Ferragamos.

"What took you so long?" asked Sam as the door closed behind her. Sam was perched on top of the marble vanity in the anteroom, flipping through a copy of *Money* magazine. "I didn't even make it through the appetizer."

Martie grimaced and waved her hands in the air. "I thought you quit smoking."

"I did," said Sam, "but I started again the day you said you'd marry that bozo."

"Give me a break, Sam," Martie warned as she sat down on one of those wrought-iron powder room chairs scaled for Munchkins. "I just suffered through an hour listening to Margaret complain about the food, the lighting, the music and the air-conditioning."

Sam stubbed out her cigarette in a crystal ashtray. "Think of all the wonderful holidays in your future, little sister. You and Jason and Margaret sitting around the fireplace, complaining about the pâté and truffles."

"I love you, Sam, but right now I don't feel like listening to you."

"You're making a mistake. You know it, I know it, Jason probably knows it."

"Sam—"

"A huge mistake," Sam continued, ignoring Martie's protests. "But it's not too late to do something about it."

"I don't want to do anything about it. I'm marrying Jason of my own free will."

"Right. And Daddy's insanity has nothing to do with it."

Martie rested her forehead against the cool glass of the mirror and looked at her sister's reflection. "What do you want me to say?"

"The truth," said Sam. "That the only reason you're going to marry Jason is to keep your inheritance."

Martie swung around to face her sister head-on. "It could be worse," she said, trying to lighten the moment with a grin. "I could be marrying Jason for *his* inheritance."

Sam obviously found no humor in her statement. "Just because Daddy's temporarily lost his marbles is no reason you have to go along with it. *I* certainly don't intend to marry someone I don't love just to keep an inheritance."

"It would mean your job," Martie said. "I thought you loved what you do." Sam had made a solid place for herself in the corporate offices of Wilde & Daughters Ltd. Conventional wisdom said she would be CFO by her fortieth birthday.

"I love the company as much as you do," Sam said, "but I'll take my skills somewhere else if I have to."

"It's different for me," Martie said. "I'm an artist. My vision is tied in with the company."

"Hogwash," said Sam. "There's more to this ridiculous sham of an engagement than that."

"Jason and I have an understanding," Martie said, aware of how feeble her explanation sounded. "We want the same things from life."

"Please," Sam said, tossing the magazine aside as she slid off the counter. "If you can't be honest with me, at least be honest with yourself. Marriage is tough enough, Martie. If you don't love him, don't marry him. No amount of money is worth that."

With that, Sam stalked from the room, leaving Martie alone in the ladies' room.

You're right, Sam, Martie thought as she looked at her reflection in the mirror. That was not the face of a woman in love; it was the face of a woman about to make the biggest mistake of her life.

For a long time after Trask's death, she'd blamed Lucky, calling him a heartless monster who wouldn't understand true love unless it tapped him on the shoulder and handed him a business card.

And her words had found their target. More than Martie's heart had been broken that spring; in a way, she thought, Lucky's had been, as well.

Lucky had begun to age that long-ago summer, as if some unseen hand had etched the lines in his face a little deeper, dimmed the sparkle in his eyes. But she'd been too hurt and angry to care. Their relationship had never recovered.

Not even time had dulled the memory of the wonder she'd glimpsed in Trask's arms, and she'd known even then that she'd never experience anything so glorious again.

In a way, it no longer mattered. She was older. She'd convinced herself she wanted different things. Wilde & Daughters Ltd. was her lover now. She'd learned to take all her passion, all her pain, and throw it headlong into her designs.

They said she was a genius, that talent like hers came along only once in every generation, and that those who came after would have to live up to the standard she'd set.

She was her father's daughter in every way but blood, and she had earned her rightful place at his side, and she would let nothing and no one, not even Lucky, take it away from her.

Marry or lose your inheritance.

If marrying Jason was what it took to hold on to her place at Wilde & Daughters, then she'd marry him, even if they did have about as much chemistry as a pair of puppies in a basket.

But that's not the real reason you're doing this, Martie. Sam is right. You haven't been honest... not even with yourself.

She was tired of being alone, tired of pretending she was happy, tired of dreaming things that could never come true. Lucky's ultimatum had been a catalyst, and she was glad of it. It was time to put the past aside and get on with her future.

Her future with Jason Blackburn.

"Jason's a great guy," one of her old high school classmates had said to her earlier, over the hors d'oeuvres. "Rich. Good-looking. You could do a lot worse."

Martie couldn't deny that last statement. She supposed she could have ended up engaged to a gun-toting psychopath who thought *Silence of the Lambs* was a great date movie. You could *always* do worse, but why was it nobody ever mentioned the fact that just maybe you might do *better?*

Jason was every bit as bad as she was when the topic was matrimony. He didn't even care that together they had the combined pulse rate of your average garden snail. Martie was bright, friendly and successful. He could trot her out for business dinners and cocktail parties and never have to worry that she'd embarrass him.

A marriage of convenience, in every sense of the phrase. She didn't have to worry about love or passion. When you expected nothing but a common address and a certain degree of loyalty, you didn't have to worry about a broken heart.

And if some people, like Sam, thought she was selling herself short—well, that was their problem.

So why did the whole thing suddenly make her feel claustrophobic, as if she'd been locked away in a tiny room and could only glimpse the rest of the world through a small, locked window?

You know why, she thought. Something about that man standing near the ATM in Fiesta had broken through a decade of defenses and awakened feelings in her she'd thought long dead. That heated rush of the blood, the sense that anything was possible . . . maybe even love.

Tonight she'd remembered how it could be between a man and a woman, and she was no longer certain she could settle for anything less.

TRASK HAD BEEN HERE forty-seven minutes, cruising the perimeter of the room, looking for Wilde, with nothing on his mind but the disaster that was barreling down on the lot of them when he saw her again.

She sat at the head table, drooping over her salad like a wilted lettuce leaf. Again the sight of her hit him like a battering ram to the gut. She'd looked happier in the supermarket line than she did sitting across from the guy she planned to marry.

He didn't know whether to feel sorrier for her or for himself.

As far as he could see, the future bridegroom hadn't spent more than thirty seconds talking to Martie since Trask got there. In fact, it looked like the guy was conducting a business meeting right there at the dinner table, while she sank lower in her chair.

Not that it was any of his business. She'd stopped being his business when he walked out the door ten years ago and into another life. He had no rights over her. She could marry Elvis's ghost, or the guy she was sitting next to, or become a cloistered nun. It made no difference.

The only thing he cared about was finding her father.

THE ORCHESTRA segued into the sinuous rhythm of the tango. Martie tried to catch Jason's attention but he was oblivious of everything but the conversation he was having with one of Lucky's golfing buddies.

She supposed she should be grateful. If she stood up, everyone would see the gigantic run that was working its way up to the waistband of her panty hose. Two pairs in one night. That had to be some kind of record.

Not to mention the record she was setting for chocolate consumption. The mousse wasn't bad, but the soufflé was to die for. If that tango didn't hurry up and finish, she might actually plow her way through the entire tray.

She was considering a piece of seven-layer cake when she saw him, moving toward her in the shadows. He wore a tux easily, as if he'd been born with the knowledge that he was a cut above mere mortals.

Something about the width of his shoulders, the way he held himself, put her in mind of the man from Fiesta, but that was impossible. That man had worn jeans and a T-shirt and looked like he'd be at home on the back of a Harley. He'd exuded danger from every pore.

This man exuded danger, too, but it was a different kind. More subtle and, in its own way, more ominous.

Run, a voice inside her heart screamed. *Get up from the table and run as fast and as far as you can.*

She pushed back her chair and stood up.

"I'm going to the ladies' room," she announced to Jason.

Jason nodded in her direction, but he didn't miss a beat of his conversation. It was her eighth visit to the bathroom since she'd arrived. You would think somebody might notice and recommend a good urologist. She paused for a moment, waiting for him to acknowledge her presence, and when he didn't, she lifted her chin and started for the door.

"The next dance is mine," said a male voice behind her.

Heat gathered deep inside her chest. Rough honey, she thought. The kind of voice that took years of smoke-filled rooms, whiskey chasers and hard living to acquire. She'd never heard a voice quite like that before, and yet there was something vaguely familiar about the sound.

Here was trouble. Sweet, seductive trouble. If she turned around and met his eyes, she was done for.

Shoulders straight, chin high, she continued toward the bathroom.

"You should be dancing." He fell into step behind her. Her entire body registered his presence. "This is your party, isn't it?"

She pointed across the room. "My cousin Linda's not dancing. Why don't you ask her?"

"Because I'm asking you."

"And I'm refusing."

"If you're worried about old Jason, I don't think he'd mind. He doesn't look like he's much for the tango."

He was probably right about that. Jason wouldn't care if she ran off to Tahiti, as long as she was discreet about it. Still, she didn't need to have her nose rubbed in that fact.

She whirled around. "Let me see your invitation." She'd spent endless hours working on the guest list with Lucky and her future mother-in-law, and she knew every name on it. If his name was on the list, she'd recognize it, and if not, she'd make sure he got to know one of their security guards, up close and personal.

"They collected the invitations at the door."

She opened her mouth to protest, then remembered seeing security guards, impeccably dressed in dinner jackets, doing exactly that.

"Who invited you?" she demanded.

He smiled, but the forbidding expression in his eyes didn't change. "Your father is an old friend of mine."

Dangerous, she thought, resisting the urge to take a step back. *This man isn't anybody's friend.* But still there was something, some elemental force, that drew her closer, even as she longed to move away.

"You're saying Daddy invited you?"

"Who else?" He made a show of glancing around the ballroom. "So where is Lucky?"

"He's not here."

"I can see that. Where is he?"

She resisted the urge to wrap her arms about her chest in a classic posture of self-defense. "He won't be joining us tonight."

"Protesting your choice of groom?"

"That's not funny."

He knows, she thought. *He knows I don't love Jason.* His gaze burned into her, making her feel more naked than if he'd stripped her of all her clothes.

She cleared her throat with a nervous little cough that sounded more like a Chihuahua's sneeze. "Look, since his heart attack, Daddy hasn't..."

HER WORDS struck him in the center of his chest, hard as a blow. A heart attack, she'd said. Lucky was a bear of a man who dominated a room just by walking into it. He couldn't imagine Lucky felled by anything so fallibly human.

A rush of emotion, dark and powerful, flooded his brain. Lucky Wilde was mortal.

Who would have thought it?

"He isn't—?" He couldn't finish the sentence.

She looked at him curiously, and then her gaze seemed to soften. "Thank God for the doctors at University. They just about brought him back from the dead. He's doing great now, but wasn't quite up to partying. I wanted to postpone things until he was completely recovered, but he insisted we go ahead with the plans."

"So where is he?"

"At the ranch."

"Where is that?"

Her expression grew more guarded. "If you were really a good friend of my father's, you wouldn't have to ask me that question."

"Go ahead," he said, flashing a facsimile of a smile. "Do me a favor and refresh my memory."

"This is a ridiculous conversation," she said, turning away. "If you'll excuse me—"

He grabbed her wrist. "I need to speak to your father."

His words floated toward her on a warm sea of pure sexual energy. The moment he touched her, she could feel every cell and fiber of her being clicking on like a light switch.

The same way it had with Trask.

It was the most exhilarating, intoxicating, terrifying feeling she'd ever had, and she wanted it to stop immediately.

She looked down at her wrist, then pointedly up at him. "Let go of me."

"Not until you tell me where Lucky's hiding."

"Hiding?" She pulled her arm away. "He's not hiding. I told you, he's at the ranch."

The Lucky Wilde that Trask had known would have moved heaven and earth to be at his daughter's side for her engagement party. Alarm bells had gone off in his head the second Martie said that Lucky had flatlined. If that was common knowledge, his enemies might be closer to implementing phase two than he'd figured.

The one thing he was sure about was that Martie wasn't lying to him. After all these years, she still didn't know how to lie. It was good to know that somewhere in the world, someone was capable of telling the plain, unvarnished truth.

Even Lucky Wilde hadn't managed that. He'd lived between two worlds, torn between the family he loved and the danger he craved. The need to walk on the edge was a call too seductive to resist.

Lucky had known that, and now Trask did, as well.

He wasn't more than a half day ahead of the people who wanted to turn him into a human killing machine, and this time Trask was damn sure they'd do the job right. He had to find Lucky, and fast.

He looked at Martie. She was watching him intently, her aqua eyes wide and curious and more than a little angry. She didn't have a clue that the fierce man with the scarred face who stood in front of her was the same man who'd given her his heart.

Look into my eyes, Martie. See me.

But she didn't. He was surprised how much it hurt.

It's better that way, he told himself. He had no time for complications and no stomach for confrontation.

No, he didn't want anything from Martie except directions to the ranch. The music around them grew louder. More insistent. So did he. "One dance." He smiled down at her. "For your father."

"You're very persistent."

He took another step toward her. She still smelled like springtime and forgotten dreams.

"One dance," he said. "That's not asking for so much, is it?"

Chapter Seven

His touch electrified her, with a cross between pleasure and pain that stole her breath. He drew her toward him, placing the flat of his left hand against the small of her back. Her mind went blank as sensations overlapped each other so rapidly that she couldn't put a name to them, but they were familiar. Almost frighteningly so.

The music grew more insistent, urging her toward something both compelling and unknowable, and she felt her bones begin to melt.

He knew what he was about, this stranger did. Strong, commanding, the ultimate lover, as he led her through the dance of seduction and surrender.

Surrender?

Get a grip, Martie. This is the guy from the supermarket. The one in the jeans and T-shirt who'd looked like he was casing the joint for an easy target. Although she had to admit there was nothing of that guy visible in the man who stood before her now.

"So what were you doing in Fiesta?" she asked.

"What's Fiesta?"

"Don't patronize me. I saw you standing by the teller machine. You were wearing jeans and a white T-shirt and you looked like you were about to mug somebody."

"You must have me confused with somebody else."

"No, I don't think I do. You're—" God help her, but she'd almost told him he was too dangerous-looking to forget. "I remember faces."

"So do I, and if I'd seen yours, I would remember."

Heat flooded her cheeks. She'd always been a sucker for cheap compliments. "Thank you, but I know I saw you." He wasn't any better at feigning innocence than she was at feigning stupidity.

"You saw someone who looked like me."

"Right down to the scars on your face?"

The light of combat was in his eyes. "Blunt, aren't you?"

"When necessary."

"They say everyone has a twin. Looks like you found mine at Festival."

"Fiesta."

He grinned. "See? I don't even know the name of the place."

"That doesn't prove anything." She considered him carefully. "You might be a great liar."

"Good," he said modestly. "Not great."

There was an edginess about him that went beyond his tone of voice. She could feel it in the coiled strength of the arms that held her, the sense of leashed power.

Of desperation.

What a strange thought. She tried to brush it away, but the notion lingered, gathering strength and adding to her sense of unease. She needed to get away while she still could.

"This has been lovely, but—" He drew her closer as the music grew hotter. "Maybe we shouldn't—"

"Quiet." The steps were quick and unfamiliar, but it didn't seem to matter. The laws of gravity no longer applied. He moved her across the floor as if they'd been dancing together for years, as if their bodies shared an intimate history she couldn't even imagine.

I want you, she thought, looking up at the stranger who held her against his body as if she belonged there. She didn't know him, she probably wouldn't like him if she did, but she wanted him more than she'd wanted anything in years.

She wanted to run her hands across his chest, rip open his shirt and press her mouth against his skin; she wanted to listen to his heart beating beneath her ear, breathe in his smell until she was drunk on the sight and scent and sound of him.

And, dear God, his smell! Masculine, powerful, about as dangerous as it came.

She stumbled, and his grip tightened, drawing her back into the rhythm of the dance so quickly that she didn't lose the beat. Their eyes met. Her heart, the same heart that had remained resolutely untouched for the past ten years, ached with long- ing for something she'd thought she could live without.

This is wrong. You can't feel this way about a stranger.

The last time she'd felt this way, she'd been a seventeen-year-old girl who believed in happily- ever-after. She wasn't seventeen any longer, and she knew that happy endings rarely happened in real life.

This wasn't the kind of man you made a life with, the kind of man who fed kids and diapered babies and held you when you cried.

Jason might not be Mr. Right, but he was a safer bet than the man who held her in his arms. That should count for something.

But it didn't.

They stood there in the middle of the dance floor, with the lights and the music and the laughter washing over them, and for one fierce instant she wished it never had to end, that she could spend the rest of her life in his arms.

He stopped dancing.

She swayed against him, a moth drawn to the flame.

Kiss me, she thought, *and I'll never ask for anything else again.*

The tango dropped down into a slow dance, the kind that evoked dark rooms and heated whispers. The French doors were only thirty feet away. She knew they led out onto a patio that was shielded from prying eyes by lush bougainvillea and the lacy fronds of mimosa and willows.

You've lost your mind, Martie! You can't go out onto the patio with this guy.

He wasn't one of her crowd of nice men who knew how to take no for an answer. This man was dancing her out onto the patio for a reason, and he wasn't going to content himself with hand-holding or murmuring sweet nothings in her shell-like ear.

A fierce exultation erupted deep in the pit of her stomach, as thrilling as it was terrifying. She knew what would happen between them out there, knew it the way she knew her own face in the mirror each morning. He would hold her against his chest, his strong arms pinning her close to his body, his sweet breath hot on her skin. His big hands would cradle her hips, then follow the inward curve of her waist up and up until he cupped the fullness of her breasts in his palms.

She began to tremble with anticipation. All around them, people laughed and danced and toasted to her future with Jason, while not one of them realized that each day she came closer to making the biggest mistake of her life.

This was the way she should feel, all wild and eager, as if every step she'd ever taken, every move she'd ever made, had brought her to this time and place. This was the way she'd felt all those years ago, the way she'd thought she would never feel again.

They slipped outside, closing the French doors behind them. Closing out the world. The sudden absence of noise and music disoriented her. How loud her heart sounded. How vulnerable. Could he hear the way her breath caught in her throat each time she looked at him? Did longing have a sound?

Tiny white lights twinkled from the branches of the forsythia. A thin crescent moon hung suspended in the ebony sky, silver against jet. A gentle wind ruffled her bangs like a caress, and he reached out to smooth the strands back into place. She longed to turn her face into the palm of his hand, breathe deeply of his smell, let his warmth become part of her heart and soul, if only for a moment.

He traced the outline of her mouth with his thumb, the fleshy pad of his finger urging her lips apart. Eyes half-closed, dizzy with madness, she touched him with the tip of her tongue, savoring the salty taste of his skin.

The sound he made was low, almost animal in its intensity, a deep, growling moan that made her want to shout with joy that she had this power over him. She drew him into her mouth, nipping at him, wanting to own him as he already owned her.

It wasn't enough. It couldn't possibly be enough. But, dear God, it was more than she'd ever dreamed possible.

HE CUPPED the back of her head with his other hand, maintaining his distance but somehow joining them together. He wanted to pull her up against him until she felt him, hard and ready to burst, pressing against her mound. He wanted to slide his hand under her skirt and feel her heat, moist and sweet, against his fingers. He wanted to watch her eyes widen as he parted her, then hear her cry of pleasure as he took her, hard and fast, standing in the shadows of the bougainvillea with no one to see them but the moon.

She opened her eyes, those magnificent aqua eyes, and gave him a look of such pure, sweet hunger that he forgot everything else but the siren call of the blood.

For her it was like stepping off the edge of a cliff and discovering that she could fly. He drew her into his arms, and her heart soared high above the stars. *Yes!* That one word drowned out even the wild pulse of her heart. This was the man she'd been destined to find, the one she was meant to be with forever.

His hand swept lightly across the curve of her breasts, and she could feel her nipples pebbling against the fabric of her dress. He trailed down the inward curve of her waist, the flare of her hip, the length of her thigh, and she gasped as he caught the hem of her skirt between his fingers and inched it up slowly. She burned each place he touched, tiny brushfires leaping to life from his fingertips.

"Panty hose," he said, against her mouth. "Damn."

He cupped her with his hand, and the rasp of his rough skin against the fragile nylon seemed unbearably erotic. Her mind was a wild jumble of thoughts, a tangle of sensations. She wanted him to push her skirt up around her hips and rip the hose from her body so that he could touch her the way she needed to be touched. She didn't want to talk. She didn't need to know his name. Later on, she would want all of that and more, but not now.

Now was about sensation. The violent rush of the blood that defied reason and shattered sanity and made her wildly, passionately, glad to be alive and in this place at this moment with this man.

Whoever he might turn out to be.

SHE MOANED low in her throat, a soft sound of surrender that brought him to the brink. And the hell of it was, she didn't even know what she'd done.

But he knew. It was the wrong time and the wrong place and it sure as hell was the wrong woman, but what was happening between them couldn't be denied. He told himself it was because it had been a lifetime since he'd held a woman, that the fire burning inside him could be extinguished between any willing pair of thighs, that there was nothing special or magical about the woman he held in his arms. But it was a lie.

She was his for the taking. She quivered against his hand, her wet heat palpable through the fragile barrier of nylon and lace. He could rip it away, lift her by the hips, then lower her onto his hard shaft, sinking deep into her body until he found his release. He was hard and she was ready and it wouldn't take long for a shattering climax to flatten them both.

But it wouldn't be enough. It would only be the start of something he couldn't finish and didn't have the right to start.

She was so damn sweet. Sweeter than the dreams he had that could never come true. Somehow the world hadn't found her yet. She was bright and sharp-tongued and nobody's fool, but an air of hallowed innocence wreathed her lovely face, like the glow around one of Raphael's angels. He pulled her up close against him, letting her feel what she was doing to him, ignoring the sharp stab of pain between his third rib and his spine. Her wide aqua eyes fluttered open and she smiled up at him, and in that instant he was lost, body and soul and heart.

"You know where this is going, don't you?" His voice was rough with desire.

She nodded, her cap of silky hair shimmering in the moonlight. "You're going to make love to me."

"Wrong," he whispered. "We're going to make love to each other."

Hard and fast the first time around, then slow and easy and all night. He knew how she would sound, how she would taste, how she'd be all open and ready and hungry for him. For ten years she'd been burned into his memory, and nothing—not even death—had made him forget.

With a growl of despair, he reached for her arm and pulled her deeper into the darkness. Cupping her face, he claimed her mouth, plundering it with long, slow, voluptuous strokes of his tongue, claiming her the way no man had ever done before... the way no other man ever would.

The pain inside him was great, and growing greater. Sharp arcs of it between his ribs and spine. He had to stop, had to push her away before it was too late. Before she was drawn into something from which there was no escape.

"You belong in there," he said, gesturing toward the glittering ballroom.

"I don't know where I belong," she said, as a feeling of desperation rose inside her chest. "I've never known." She felt as if she'd been searching her entire life for this man, and she wasn't about to let him go.

"Never?"

"Only once," she whispered, "but it was a long time ago..."

The shadows played against the hard angles of his face. The crescent-shaped scar on his cheek only added to his dangerous allure. Scarcely breathing, she reached up to touch him, then jumped as her fingertips made contact with his skin.

He met her eyes. Even in the darkness, she could see the sadness in them.

This is it, she thought, trembling. *This is when my life starts again.*

"Martina." Jason's voice rang out in the warm night air.

The stranger met her eyes. "Don't marry him," he said. "Just promise me you won't marry him."

"Who are you? Tell me who you are, and I'll—"

But it was too late. He vaulted the railing and vanished into the night as Jason reached her side.

"There you are, Martina. I thought I heard you out here."

She wondered how much Jason had seen. He sounded the way he always sounded, like a high-rent car dealer about to cement a sale. She kept her back to him as she waited for the high spots of color to fade from her cheeks.

"I've been looking for you," he said.

"Well, now you've found me," she said brightly, turning to face him. "Is your business meeting over?"

He gave her his patented corner-office-with-a-window grin. "Nailed another one!" He couldn't keep the note of triumph from his voice. "Brilliant move, asking Bates Richardson to the party."

We're alone in the moonlight, Jason. Wouldn't you rather kiss me than talk business? "Far be it from me to stand in the way of making a deal."

He draped an arm about her shoulders in a gesture more companionable than romantic. Her skin barely registered his touch. "That's what I've always liked about you, darlin'. You know what's important in life."

"Yes," she said, thinking about the way she'd felt in the arms of a stranger. "Maybe I do, at that."

HE WATCHED HER from the darkness as she slipped her arm through her fiancé's and walked back inside the ballroom. He wanted to vault the railing, sweep her up into his arms and take her away with him. Too bad the only place he could take her was that sleazy motel near the highway.

It hadn't always been that way, he thought as he stepped deeper into the shadows he called home. He'd been born into a world more rarefied than hers, but she'd had something he didn't: a family who loved her.

He tensed at a sound to his left, crouching low to the ground. Music floated toward him from the ballroom. Laughter shot sparks into the air. He waited for the crack of a rifle shot or the glint of a knife blade whizzing his way, but none came. The ordinary sounds of a spring evening took on a different cast when you were running for your life.

Ten years was a long time. She wasn't a girl any longer, looking up at him through tangled lashes. She was successful in her own right. Her jewelry designs were the engine that would power Wilde & Daughters into the next century. She had family and friends who loved her, a man she intended to marry, but in her eyes he still saw the shadow of the middle daughter.

The one everybody forgot.

Don't worry, sweetheart, he thought as he turned away from the sounds of celebration. *Nobody could forget you now.*

Chapter Eight

An hour later, Martie and Jason stood beneath the porte cochere and waited for Hank to bring the limo around.

"Are you sure you don't want me to see you home?" Jason asked.

She shook her head. "It's out of your way. Besides, Daddy's limo is here. I might as well use it."

Jason hesitated, as if he were debating the wisdom of pressing the matter, and she withheld a sigh. Jason wasn't about to challenge her decision on this, or anything else, for that matter. Not when he was this close to marrying one of Lucky Wilde's daughters.

Last week she'd believed compliance to be the most important trait in a future husband, but now she found herself longing for a little fire, the sense that in a battle of wills she just might have found her match.

Like your tango partner? He'd never let you get away with a stunt like this. If she couldn't share a car with Jason, what on earth made her believe she could share his bed?

"Martie." Jason sounded petulant. "You're not listening."

"There's Hank with the car." She pressed a quick kiss to his smooth cheek. "Talk to you tomorrow."

She leapt into the back seat before Hank had a chance to get out and open the door. The welcoming sound of a Judds oldie enveloped her in its arms.

"You're too fast for me, Miss Martie," Hank said, twisting around to meet her eyes. "Gonna make me look bad."

"Never that," she said with real fondness. "I'm just eager to get home."

Hank waited, tapping his forefinger against the wheel to the rhythm of Wynonna's glorious voice. "Sure taking his sweet time, isn't he?"

"Who?"

"Your intended. Why in tarnation is he just standin' there?"

She swiveled around and peered through the back window. Jason stood on the curb, hands in his pockets, looking for all the world like a kid about to throw a temper tantrum. She felt as if she'd escaped a fate worse than death. "He's not coming with us, Hank. It's just me."

Hank opened his mouth to say something, but obviously thought better of it. That judgment was one of the reasons he'd been her father's driver for more than twenty years. Minutes later, the limo merged onto the highway, and Jason was left behind.

She kicked off her shoes and curled her legs beneath her. No point worrying about the panty hose. They were already shot. Or were they? She extended her right leg and frowned. She could have sworn a huge run had destroyed this pair, too, but they'd looked just fine.

"Oh, who cares?" she mumbled, curling up again. A run, or the lack of one, was the least of her worries.

"You okay back there, Miss Martie?" Hank asked as they drove across town. "You're real quiet tonight. All partied out?"

"Just tired, Hank, that's all."

"Not cryin', are you? If that boyfriend of yours kicked up a fuss, I'll go back there and—"

"Jason didn't do anything, Hank. I'm the one who kicked up the fuss."

"Good," said Hank, as Wynonna gave way to early Loretta. "Gotta keep those rich boys in line, I always say."

She settled back in the darkness. Alone on the night of her engagement party. Was it any wonder Hank kept glancing at her in the rearview mirror? She flashed on a vision of herself, all decked out in her bridal gown, home alone on her wedding night while Jason cut a business deal with one of their guests.

The sad part was, she liked that scenario better than the more traditional one.

Something had to give, she thought, closing her eyes. She would have to sit down with her father and tell him the truth, that she'd rather be alone the rest of her days than be married to Jason. Maybe next week she'd drive up to the ranch and have a heart-to-heart with him, tell him that she'd do anything to remain part of Wilde & Daughters.

Everything, that was, except commit marriage.

"You want me to walk you inside?" Hank asked as the limo rolled to a stop in front of the guest house, where she'd been living since the day Trask Benedict died.

She shook her head. "I'll be fine."

The guest house was situated on the far side of the Wilde property. Hidden from sight by a grove of live oak trees, it was protected by the same sophisticated security system that Lucky employed up at the main house. "The White House doesn't have a system this good," her father liked to brag. "A fire ant can't get inside without setting off an alarm.''

Lucky wasn't exaggerating. Twice Martie had brought out the entire Houston police force when she punched in the wrong access code. Fortunately, she had no such trouble tonight. She waved to Hank, who had been waiting at the foot of the driveway, then stepped inside.

The heavy steel-cored door swung closed behind her. The locks clicked into place automatically.

The low hum of the electronic sensors buzzed.

And then a hand reached out of the darkness and clamped itself over her mouth.

''Scream,'' said a familiar rough-honey voice, ''and it's all over.''

FIRST SHE BIT HIS FINGER.

And *then* she screamed.

''Damn it!'' That wonderful voice turned to gravel as he drew back in surprise and—she fervently hoped—pain.

She didn't waste a minute. She headed for the front door as fast as her three-inch heels would carry her, but he grabbed her before she could punch in the first number of the emergency code.

''It's been disconnected,'' he said as he swept her off her feet and dragged her, kicking wildly, toward the back of the house.

"Liar!" She swung out with her fists and managed to clip him in the side of the head. "It worked a minute ago."

"Only because I set it up that way."

He sat her down hard on a ladder-back chair in the kitchen, then pulled it closer to him. Less than three hours ago she'd stood in the shadows with this man, on fire for his touch. She'd been dizzy with longing, ready to toss aside every moral standard she held dear, all because it felt so right to be in his arms.

He was a con man, all right, and the con was older than time.

She'd never let him know that she'd actually fallen for it. Lifting her chin, she met his eyes. "If you want jewelry, you can have it. We're insured." She gestured toward the huge diamond ring on her left hand. "Here. Take it."

"Sentimental, aren't you?" The expression in his eyes spoke volume. "I thought that was your engagement ring."

"It is," she said, as heat flooded her cheeks. "Excuse me if I'd rather not die for a piece of jewelry."

He pulled a length of cord from the inside pocket of his tuxedo jacket. "I'm not interested in your jewelry."

The memory of how she'd felt in his arms caused a thrill to race up her spine. "This house is wired with the most elaborate security system on the face of the earth. Right now your face is being transmitted to every police station in Houston."

"Wrong again," he said, stretching the cord between his hands. "I bypassed the system."

"That's impossible."

"Nothing's impossible." He looped the cord around her wrists. "I'm here, aren't I?"

"What's that supposed to mean?"

"Your security system," he said blandly. "You thought it was foolproof."

She tried to keep her wrists an inch apart so that she'd have some room to maneuver, but he was too clever for that. He bound her hands tightly together. No doubt he'd had a lot of practice.

"*I* don't even know everything this cottage is equipped with," she said, trying to sound cool and calm. "Trust me, the authorities will show up any minute."

"We'll be gone by the time they get here."

"What do you mean, we? I'm not going anywhere with you."

"You're coming with me." He had the bone-deep self-confidence of a man who wasn't accustomed to hearing the word *no*. "If I leave you here, they'll kill you."

"Trust me," she said. "The only person who wants to kill me is my cleaning lady." And that was just on alternate Wednesdays.

"They won't think twice about blowing you away."

"So far, you're the only one I'm afraid of."

"Take me to Lucky, and you can forget this ever happened."

"If you don't know where Lucky is, I'm certainly not going to tell you. He needs peace and quiet."

"If you want to see him alive again, you'll take me to him."

Her hands were tied, but her ankles weren't. She kicked him in the left shin with the pointy toe of one of her high-heeled shoes.

If she'd hurt him, it didn't show. "Okay, Princess, one more time—where's your father?"

She glared up at him, but said nothing. *What on earth have you gotten yourself into, Daddy?* Rambo-in-a-tux didn't look like he was planning to make a social call.

The overhead light flickered, then died. She jumped in alarm, the chair tilted, and she fell hard against his hip. He caught her before she hit the ground, cradling both her and the chair against his body. *You can trust him,* whispered a little voice. *He's telling you the truth.*

"We've got trouble," he said, his voice low. "They've found us."

"We're in the kitchen!" she screamed, not one to believe those little voices when the evidence said otherwise. "Hurry, before he—"

Kissed her?

TRASK KISSED HER for the second time that night.

Her warm, full mouth was as sweet as he remembered. Too bad she was trying to scream the house down with it.

"You don't want them to find you," he murmured against her lips.

She twisted in his arms, threw back her head, then opened her mouth wide to let out another howl.

He liked to think he was as tough and heartless as they came, but dying had done something to him, softened him in ways he still didn't understand. He hated the look of fear behind her anger, didn't want to be the reason for it.

"Come on," he said, untying her wrists. "Let's get out while we still can."

"I'm not going anywhere with you."

He grabbed her by the shoulders and forced her to meet his eyes. "Those guys out there aren't your friends, and they sure as hell aren't mine. They're out to get me, and they'd like to get your father, too, and if they have to kill you to do it, then those are the breaks. Now let's move it."

"I'll take my chances here."

"This isn't a multiple-choice quiz. You're coming with me."

He grabbed her wrist. The rest of her body followed along with it.

"Get down," he ordered, ducking below the countertop. "Stay out of sight."

"Why should I—"

The window shattered in an explosion of glass. She hit the ground, visions of a SWAT team dancing in her head.

"Stay flat." His tone brooked no argument.

"Don't worry." She had no desire to have her hair reparted by a semiautomatic. "Who are you? Why are they after you?"

"The less you know about it, the easier it'll go for you."

"You're scaring me."

He shot her a sideways glance. "Good. If you're scared, you might make it."

A second bullet whizzed overhead, piercing the spice cabinet over the stove. The smell of gunpowder and garlic salt was memorable.

"If we're going to die together on my kitchen floor, the least you can do is tell me what's going on."

"I have something they want."

"And they're willing to kill you for it?"

He nodded. "And they're willing to kill *you*. If they have to."

"This doesn't make any sense."

He flattened himself out like a limbo dancer, pushing away shards of glass from broken spice bottles. "It doesn't have to. Just do what I tell you, and you'll get out of this alive."

"Getting out of here alive wasn't a problem until you showed up." Five minutes ago, the only thing she'd wanted to get out of was this darned spangled dress.

"Is there another way out?"

She pointed toward an archway at the rear of the kitchen. "The mudroom opens onto the side yard."

They inched their way across the floor like garden snakes. He was considerably better at it than she was, a fact that annoyed her out of all proportion.

He stopped slithering at the mudroom. "What's this?"

"That's Sly's door."

"Who's Sly?"

"My cat." Actually, he belonged to Carlota, the housekeeper, but he'd decided to live in both houses.

"You could drive a semi through that flap."

"Sly has a bit of a weight problem."

"Great," he said, eyeing the opening. "Now all we have to do is get our butts through it and we're out of here."

"I'm not going through a cat door."

"The hell you're not."

"The spirit's willing, but the hips will never make it."

"I'll push you."

"Touch me once and you'll wish your friends had been better shots."

"Count of three, Princess." His tone was as menacing as the expression in his eyes. A few hours ago, she'd been willing to give herself to him, body and soul. Now the thought made her shiver.

"This is insane. I..."

"One."

"...absolutely refuse to..."

"Two."

"...act like a total..."

"Three."

His hands reached for her derriere and suddenly Sly's cat door didn't look half as impossible as it had a second before. She scrunched down and wiggled her way through the opening, leaving a sparkling trail of bugle beads behind.

What a ridiculous situation to be in. If she weren't so terrified, she'd laugh at the absurdity of waiting for Mr. Breaking and Entering to work his broad shoulders through a cat door. It didn't take a structural engineer to know the odds were against him.

She felt exposed, vulnerable, as if she'd been dropped in the middle of a foreign landscape. They were out there somewhere, aiming their guns right in her direction. She pressed herself flatter on the damp grass, wishing she'd worn a plain black dress that didn't glitter in the moonlight like a neon sign.

"Martie!" Hank's voice tore through the stillness. "Where you hidin'?"

The man was squishing his way through the wet grass like a wild boar. He couldn't be a better target if he had a bull's-eye painted across the back of his jacket.

"Get down, Hank!" she cried out. "They've got guns!"

"Hell, yes, they've got guns. Damn fool McClellan boys are out shooting squirrels."

Squirrels? That was disgusting. She sat up. No bullets threatened to double-pierce her earlobes. "Are you sure?"

Hank kept squishing his way toward her. "Saw Billy McClellan with my own eyes, with that BB gun his daddy gave him for Christmas. Called the police on them from the car phone."

"That wasn't a BB gun that blew out my kitchen window." Or a BB gun that had made her intruder hit the floor.

"Sure it was," said Hank, not the least bit worried. "You'd be real surprised what kind of damage a BB can do."

She'd debate the issue with him later. "Call the police," she ordered, brushing clods of dirt from her cleavage. "I've trapped an intruder inside the house."

"Those damn kids," Hank muttered as he helped her up. "Ain't enough to go hurtin' innocent animals, they gotta kick up a fuss with their neighbors."

She gestured back toward the mudroom. "That's not one of the McClellans trapped in the cat door."

Hank looked in that direction, then back again at her. "Right, Martie. That's not one of the McClellans." He was looking at her as if she'd taken leave of her senses.

She spun around. The cat door swung gently, and she noticed Sly stretched out on the flagstone path, washing his left hind paw. No sign at all of the man with the rough-honey voice.

"He was there a second ago," she said, glancing about. Trapped like the rat he was, his big broad shoulders wedged tightly in the narrow opening.

Hank frowned. "If you mean Sly, he's right there."

"I mean the intruder."

"Somebody was in your house?"

"That's what I'm trying to tell you. He was waiting for me when I got home from the party."

Hank swore, then quickly apologized. "I knew I should've walked you inside."

"You can make up for that now, Hank. He's still in there, and somebody has to capture him."

They looked at each other. Hank didn't seem any more eager to confront the man than she was.

"How do you know he's still in there?" Hank asked, shoving his hands in the pockets of his pants.

"Where else can he be? He couldn't fit through the cat door. I would have seen him if he'd come through the broken window, and I would have heard him if he'd used the front door. He has to be in there."

"Yup," said Hank, taking a step backward. "Looks like he's in there, all right."

Another second passed.

"This is weird," Martie said. "He wasn't shy about breaking in. Wouldn't you think he'd at least try to break out?"

"Maybe somethin' happened to him," Hank said. "Maybe one of those BBs..."

"I'm telling you they weren't BBs, and besides, he wasn't shot." At least she didn't think he'd been shot. Truth was, once the bullets started flying, she'd been a great deal more interested in her own physical welfare than in his.

"Real quiet in there," Hank remarked.

"I know." He was probably ripping through her closet, looking for the wall safe.

"What's he waitin' for, an invitation?"

Sirens wailed in the distance. Martie tensed, half expecting the intruder to burst through the door and run full-speed into the woods.

"Must be a dumb one," said Hank as the sirens grew closer. "Some of those guys like jail. Cheaper than paying rent."

Hank had a point, but she didn't think it applied to her intruder. He might have looked like a biker when she first saw him at Fiesta, but there was no denying he seemed comfortable in a tux. Almost as if he'd been born to wear one. Besides, she'd tried to give him her flawless seven-carat engagement ring in the platinum setting, and he'd turned it down.

"Somehow I don't think money's a problem for him," she said.

"Money's a problem for everyone," Hank said, casting her a quizzical look. "Either you don't have it but you want it, or you got it but you want more."

I wish it were that easy, Hank, she thought as the police cars roared up the curving drive.

The guy didn't want money—he wanted her father.

Chapter Nine

"What do you mean, there's no one in there?" Martie demanded a few minutes later.

"Sorry, Ms. Wilde," the young policeman said, "but there's nobody in there."

"There has to be somebody in there," she insisted, aware of Hank's eyes on her. "He was in there five minutes ago."

She would have had more respect for the policeman's opinion if he could manage to keep his eyes off her bugle-beaded breasts.

Hank glanced around the quiet living room. "He sure ain't here."

"You don't believe me, either one of you." Anger edged her voice. "He grabbed me right here in the hallway, then he tried to tie me to a kitchen chair."

The men exchanged glances. *Ditzy broad.* She didn't have to hear the words to know what they were thinking. Every time she called them out to check her security alarm, they treated her in the same condescending manner.

"I saw that, and I don't appreciate it. I know what happened."

"Nobody says you don't, Miss Martie," Hank said kindly. "Just it would help if there was some kind of evidence."

She turned to the knot of cops huddled near the front window. "I'm the evidence. You could dust me for fingerprints. His hands were all over me."

The youngest of the cops flushed. "Ma'am, there must've been something else he touched while he was here."

She opened her arms wide. "You name it, he touched it." She ticked off the items she was sure he'd handled. "Anita was in this morning to clean, so the only other prints should be hers and mine." And Anita was bonded, so her prints would be on record and easily accessible.

Hank dozed off in the easy chair while the detectives went about their business. Martie was too agitated to settle down. She paced the length of the room, replaying the entire bizarre night in her head.

You didn't tell them everything, Martie, did you?

She'd given the police a detailed description of the intruder, but she'd withheld their brief conversation about her father. She told herself that the last thing Lucky needed was to have a phalanx of

Houston's finest descend upon him while he was supposed to be recuperating, but there was more to it than that.

Was it possible that there really was a connection between the man she'd danced with and her father? She'd always sensed that behind Lucky's hail-fellow-well-met exterior lurked something darker, more complicated. Still waters ran deep, but they also ran dangerous.

She'd wait until they found a match for the fingerprints. Then she'd decide what to do next.

THE YELLOW ROSE MOTEL was situated off the highway, a run-down rattrap of a place with nothing going for it except indoor plumbing. The roof leaked, the windows were painted shut, the air conditioner sounded like a wide-bodied jet coming in for a landing at the airport a few miles away.

Damned if it wasn't the best room Trask had stayed in in a hell of a long time.

The night clerk tossed him a key without giving him a second glance. Letterman was about to do his top ten riff, and it was pretty obvious nothing short of a nuclear explosion would penetrate the guy's concentration.

Trask rounded the corner of the squat building and headed toward the squat building where he'd spend the night. Crushed cans of Lone Star littered the pathway, while a broken bottle of Southern Comfort softened the stench of urine and garbage.

Room 21 was better than he'd expected. Worn gray carpeting that had seen better days, with faded red splotches by the closet that he'd rather not speculate about. The bed was one of those narrow jobs with a coarse cotton bedspread the color of a compost heap, but it still offered better sleeping conditions than he'd known in days.

The bathroom was another story. Mildewed tiles. Rusty faucets. Chipped porcelain. He supposed it was better than nothing. He stripped off his clothes, everything but the chain with the silver ring dangling from it, and took advantage of what was available.

It probably wouldn't make much difference to Martie that he was grateful to the contents of the top drawer of her lingerie chest for the chance to take a shower. Two hundred dollars was nothing to her, but these days it was a lot to him.

He soaped himself a second time, then stood under the spray, letting the tepid water sluice over him. Yeah, he'd really come a long way from the old days, when money had been as easy to come by as trouble was now. Hard to believe there'd ever been a time when his only problem had been wondering if he'd live long enough to spend the fortune at his command.

Hell, he knew the answer to that. In the time it took him to die and come back to life again, his identity had been taken from him, his past had been obliterated, and now his future was out of his control.

And the hell of it was that PAX itself was at the center of the scheme.

Rot began at the top, and that was exactly what was happening with the highly respected organization. Since Alistair Chambers's death almost three years ago, control of international operations had been up for grabs. Everyone knew the Pacific rim was the wave of the future. Whoever managed to grab that particular brass ring was in the driver's seat for the next millennium.

The plan was simple enough to be brilliant: Replace world leaders with surgically and genetically altered duplicates who were part of the network of renegade operatives. It had already happened in two eastern European nations, and Trask had reason to believe the speaker of the House and the minority whip of the Senate were dupes. Next stop, the White House, the Pentagon, the Supreme Court. The implications were terrifying.

Viktor, PAX's old nemesis from the days when communism was their only problem, was rumored to be masterminding everything. Trask remembered hearing about Max Steel's run-in with Viktor some years back, when Viktor's plan to poison the United States's water supply had come terrifyingly close to being a reality. He also knew there'd been major trouble between Viktor and Lucky, but he'd never been able to uncover the details.

The good news was that Trask had survived the gunshot wounds he'd received in the South China Sea.

The bad news was that he'd been saved by PAX operatives who were part of Viktor's scheme.

And what they had planned for him was unthinkable.

Trask had regained consciousness in a sterile hospital room in Switzerland, with a new face, new voice, and new identity. He'd managed to cheat death, only to find himself being turned into a high-tech murder machine.

The water sputtered to a standstill, and he cursed sharply, as much at his lot in life as at the faulty shower. Tonight everything had changed, changed in ways that even death hadn't accomplished. He'd thought he could handle seeing Martie again, but he'd been wrong. It should have been easy. They'd spent only one night together. He was ten years and a thousand lifetimes past anything they'd shared.

Now she was a means to an end, and nothing more.

Martie had always been her father's favorite. Lucky loved all his daughters, but there was no denying he had a special feeling for Martie. All Trask had to do was grab her and lock her in his motel room, and her old man would pop out of hiding so fast Trask's head would spin.

Lucky was the one person on the face of the earth who would believe the story Trask had to tell. The one person Trask would trust with the whole incredible truth.

But something had happened when he saw her standing in line at the checkout, something improbable and miraculous and so gut-level right that he'd felt as if the earth had stopped turning long enough for him to remember how it felt to be alive.

And the hell of it was, it was too late.

He should have done it right then, when he had the chance, grabbed her behind the display of canned corn and forced her daddy to take his calls, but he'd been struck senseless, as if the thunderbolt of romantic legend had found him again.

Next time he saw her, he wouldn't make that mistake.

"YOU LOOK TERRIBLE," Estelle Ross said when Martie showed up at work the next morning. Estelle was a forty-seven-year-old unmarried dyed-in-the-wool romantic who believed most of womankind's ills could be cured by repeated doses of hearts, flowers and, of course, diamonds.

"Thanks a lot," Martie said, stifling a yawn. "No sleep will do that to a woman."

Estelle's brown eyes lit up behind her bright purple eyeglasses. "Be still my heart! You and Jason finally did the deed!"

"Estelle!" Martie's face burned with embarrassment. "Absolutely not."

"More's the pity," said Estelle. "It's long overdue, if you ask me. Maybe I was wrong about the two of you not having any va-voom."

"I didn't ask you," Martie pointed out. She refused to get into another analysis of which couples had va-voom and which ones didn't. "Am I the only woman on earth who thinks there's more to a relationship than sexual chemistry?"

Estelle rolled her eyes comically. "Honey, by the time I hit twenty-two I had that one figured out."

"I really hate this conversation, Estelle." *I had it figured out, too, Estelle. Ten years ago, with Trask.*

Estelle patted her on the shoulder. "Somebody has to talk to you about these things, honey, what with your mama gone all these years."

Estelle had been around as long as Martie could remember, part of the day-to-day fabric of life at Wilde & Daughters. Martie was convinced the woman carried a torch for Lucky that was as big as the state of Texas.

"You know what I'm talking about, Martie. We all saw you last night, honey. The sparks were flying like the Fourth of July."

Martie climbed up on her stool and struggled with her composure. "Sparks should fly," she said, deliberately misunderstanding. "Jason and I are engaged."

"I don't mean you and Jason. I mean you and your gorgeous tango partner." Estelle sighed. "If I were fifteen years younger and thirty pounds lighter, I would have danced him off to my apartment."

"Be my guest. I certainly don't have any claim to him. I don't even know his name."

"You don't have to pretend with me, honey. He got your motor runnin'. Nothing to be ashamed of about that."

"The man's a snake and a thief," she snapped, aware of the heat behind her words. She told the older woman an abridged version of the story. "He should be behind bars."

"Wow," said Estelle. "And the only prints they could find were yours and the cleaning lady's?"

"That's about the size of it." She retrieved her design sketches from the locked top drawer of her desk. "We won't talk about the missing two hundred dollars, will we?"

"He took your money?"

"Darn right he did."

"Then he must've left some fingerprints behind."

"Not a one," said Martie. "And I swear I saw him touch at least ten different things." Not to mention herself.

"No fingerprints?" Estelle sounded incredulous. "That doesn't seem possible."

"Well, it happened. The louse probably used my best dress to wipe them off before he left."

"Honey, he'd have to be one slick operator to be that thorough, and if he was that good, he wouldn't have left your jewelry behind."

She threw her hands into the air. "So what do you want from me, Estelle? I'm afraid I'm not up on my police procedure."

"You'd better keep your eye on Anita, that's all I'm saying." Estelle started toward the door. "And have your locks changed."

BY THREE O'CLOCK it was obvious that the day was an unqualified disaster. With a sigh, Martie locked her sketches away in the top drawer of her desk. When you couldn't even manage to set a simple solitaire in a platinum Tiffany setting without dropping the stone three times, it was time to hang up your tools and go home.

The truth was, she couldn't stop thinking about him. She peered through the loupe and saw his face staring back at her. The crescent shape of a brooch reminded her of the curving scar on his cheek. He'd broken into her cottage and stolen her money. She knew she should be bristling with anger, yet her anger was tempered with something she couldn't quite put a name to.

It's called lust, Martie, and it's frying your brain.

Okay, so maybe her hormones had done a little two-step when she first saw him by the ATM at Fiesta, and maybe her pheromones had gotten a bit addled when they tangoed, but so what? That didn't mean she was going to toss aside almost twenty-eight years of clear thinking and rational behavior in order to satisfy her libido. She'd tried that when she was seventeen, and she wasn't about to make that mistake again.

She'd spent much of the morning on the telephone, making discreet calls to the family banker, stockbroker and priest, and nothing seemed amiss. Lucky Wilde was sound of bank balance, portfolio and spirit, and before long he'd be sound of body, as well. Hadn't Dr. Ted said that Lucky needed some good old-fashioned R and R to get back on his feet again? She couldn't risk his recovery by throwing this mess in his lap and asking him to deal with it.

She slung her bag over her shoulder, then crossed the hall and tapped on Estelle's door.

"I'm calling it a day."

Estelle looked up from a thick stack of computer printouts. "A little early, isn't it?"

"Not early enough," Martie said. "I'm exhausted. I'm going to go home and lock myself inside until tomorrow morning."

Estelle shivered. "After what you went through last night, I'm surprised you'd go back to the guest house at all. You know you can always stay with me, honey, if you get scared."

"I'm too tired to be scared." All she wanted was a warm bath, a glass of wine, and a twenty-four-hour nap.

She slipped out the back door and was crossing the parking lot when she saw him leaning against a Land Rover. She froze in place, hands trembling.

He met her eyes.

Her heart leapt into her throat as a tidal wave of emotion swelled inside her heart. *He's a louse and a thief, Martie. Get a grip!*

He started toward her. There was something hauntingly familiar about the way he moved, something that tugged at a deep chord of memory that just managed to elude her. She couldn't breathe, couldn't think, couldn't do anything except stand there like the fool she was and wait for danger to come over and introduce himself.

Are you crazy, girl? Run!

She backed up a step, then two, then turned and started to run toward the rear entrance to the store. He grabbed her ten feet away from the door.

"Call your father." He drew her close in a mock embrace, a hand clamped over her mouth. "Tell him they took Andersen and DiTello. Tell him the president—"

She tried to pull away from him, but his grip was unyielding.

"Call Lucky," he repeated, his voice rough and urgent. "I'm running out of time."

He took his hand from her mouth.

"Who *are* you?" she snapped. "Why on earth should I listen to you?"

"Because you love your father and you don't want to lose him, and that's exactly what's going to happen if I don't get to him in time. I need your help."

"Why should I help you? I don't even know you."

"I'm going to find him either way, Princess. You might as well make it easy for me."

She started to laugh. "You're unbelievable," she said, shaking her head. "I don't know if you're crazy or just plain nuts."

His fierce expression never wavered. "I don't care if you think I'm a lunatic, just get me to your father before it's too late."

"Over my dead body."

"I'm not giving you a choice, Princess." He swept her off toward the car.

What was it she'd learned in self-defense class? *Never get into a car with a stranger.* "We'll call from my office phone."

"The car phone."

"I don't have a car phone," she lied.

He recited her number. She winced. Smart *and* dangerous. She was in deep trouble.

"You stand outside and I'll hand you the phone," she said as she unlocked the car door.

He didn't argue. She punched in the number at the ranch and waited.

Two rings.

Then six.

"Strange," she said. "You'd think somebody would've picked up by now."

He crouched down between her Lexus and the Mercedes next to it. "What's wrong?"

"I don't know." His tension moved along her skin like an electrical charge.

"Maybe you dialed the wrong number. Try again."

"I don't think—"

"Do it."

She dialed, then waited again as the phone at the ranch rang and rang.

"Still no answer. You'd think Carlota would pick it up." She replaced the phone in its cradle. "Oh, God...what if Daddy had another—"

"Martie!" A piercing female voice.

Unlike last night on the patio, this time Martie welcomed the interruption.

"I can't believe it's you!" A round ball of a woman was racing toward them, her big brown eyes alight with curiosity and more than a touch of malice.

"And who have we here?" CeCe Vollenweider, society wife and jewelry addict, cooed as she looked from Martie to the man who was leaning over her, trying to push his way into the car. She was one of Wilde & Daughters's biggest customers. "Now, I *know* this isn't Jason!"

With obvious reluctance, he stood up and smiled down at CeCe. "Frank Cummings," he said. "I'm an old school friend."

Frank Cummings? In a pig's eye, thought Martie. Why didn't he just say his name was John Doe?

"How interesting," CeCe drawled. Disbelief oozed from every well-tended pore. "And here I thought I knew all of your old school friends, Martie dear."

Martie was too worried about her father to be concerned with CeCe's feelings. "CeCe, I'd love to chat with you, but I'm in a rush."

CeCe's penciled-in brows arched coyly. "I'll just bet you are, darlin'. Don't you worry one bit now, kids. I won't tell a soul I saw you here."

"Frankly, CeCe, I don't particularly—"

He draped a casual arm across Martie's shoulders. "We appreciate your kindness," he said. His hazel eyes crinkled when he smiled. CeCe practically swooned at his feet. "Someone else might have misinterpreted the situation."

"There *is* no situation," Martie snapped. "I—"

CeCe laughed like the rattlesnake she was. "I know all about these things, darlin'. Jason can boil me in oil, and I won't breathe a word."

He winked at CeCe in a most outrageous fashion, and Martie considered offering him up as a human sacrifice.

"Damn you! How on earth am I going to explain this to Jason?" Martie demanded as CeCe hurried off to spread her gossip from the Galleria to Sugar Land.

"Do you really care?"

"Go to hell."

He leaned into the car across her and reached for the keys. A book of matches fell from his pocket to the floor mat on the passenger side. He paused for an instant, distracted.

It was all the time Martie needed. She threw the car into reverse. He grunted as the door slammed him in the shoulder, knocking him to the pavement.

She didn't care if he was hurt.

She didn't care if he was dead.

The only thing she cared about was finding Lucky before he did.

Chapter Ten

Martie roared into the airfield parking lot and screeched to a stop near the hangar. Her dad's plane sat out on the tarmac, all shiny and well tended. She hoped that meant Tim McKinney, his pilot, was there, too. With any luck at all, she could be at the ranch within the hour.

The old navy flier was stretched out full length on a dark green leatherette sofa with a cup of black coffee in one hand and the Houston *Post* in the other. He'd been Lucky's pilot for the past eight years, most of which had been spent jetting between Houston and the ranch, with occasional jaunts abroad.

"Been a while," Tim said, swinging his sturdy legs off the patched arm of the sofa. "Hear you had yourself some party last night."

It seemed like a hundred years ago. "I need to get to the ranch, Tim," she said, bypassing the social amenities. "As fast as possible."

Tim eyed her over the rim of his chipped red coffee mug. "You're the boss," he said easily. "Did your daddy forget somethin' up there?"

"Forget something?" Blood pounded in her ears. "I don't understand."

"I just brung him back about an hour ago. He and Carlota shut everything up tighter than a drum."

"Daddy's back in Houston?"

"Heck, yes. Said how could a body get any rest when he had himself three unmarried daughters to worry about?" He took another huge gulp of coffee. "Must be feeling pretty chipper, because he gave me the week off to go over Galveston way and see my new grandbaby."

Martie murmured the requisite congratulations, but her mind was skidding all over the place. Lucky wasn't well enough to attend her engagement party, but he was well enough to come home the day after?

Something wasn't right.

She broke the speed limit all the way between the airport and home.

"Daddy!" She ran across the foyer, almost slipping on the freshly waxed parquet floor. "Where are you?"

No answer. Her adrenaline began to surge. She peered into the formal living room, but he wasn't there. The television room was empty, as were the library and the sun-room. She was about to race up the winding staircase to the second floor when she heard a voice behind her.

"Damnation, girl! Shouldn't you be workin' on that pendant for Helen Waggoner?"

She whirled around. Her father stood in the doorway between the dining room and the foyer, and her breath caught as she looked at him. He'd always been a big bear of a man, larger than life, both in size and personality. His denim work shirt hung loosely from his bony frame, emphasizing the weight he'd lost in the hospital. His skin seemed older somehow, more lined and weathered than before. Even the sparkle in his blue eyes was subdued, as if he had toned down the wattage to conserve strength.

An odd prickling sensation brushed against her sides, but she pushed it away. Somehow the heart attack hadn't scared her as deeply as the sight of her father standing in front of her, diminished by time. He looked more fragile now than he had looked in intensive care. How could it have happened so fast?

"What on earth are you doing here, Daddy?" She flew across the room. "I thought you were supposed to be taking it easy up at the ranch." *Why weren't you at the party last night?*

"A man's not made to sit on his rump day after day, watching the sun set. Time to get back in the saddle."

She hugged him, and he was the first to end the embrace.

Don't go reading anything into it, she warned herself. He was probably just tired from the trip home. She linked her arm through his as they walked toward the sun-room at the back of the house. They'd been on easier terms since his heart attack, as if his brush with mortality had helped them to put their differences aside, if not behind them.

"Aren't you the one who said you couldn't imagine anything better than living up at the ranch full-time?"

"Saying and doing are two different things." His gray hair was neatly clipped in a straight line across the back. Lucky usually looked as if he'd lost a battle with a hedge clipper after a stay. "I'm not ready to hand over the reins to you gals yet."

There was an edge to his words, unpleasant and definitely pointed.

"Nobody said you were, Daddy." His words stung, and she tried to modulate her tone. A heart attack wasn't a common cold, and the recuperation was as much psychological as it was physical. Dr. Ted had told Martie and her sisters that Lucky might be difficult to deal with for quite a while until he was one hundred percent again.

Lucky gravitated immediately toward the wet bar in the far corner of the sun-room. "Bourbon and branch, darlin'?"

"Sam and Frankie like bourbon, Daddy. I'm the one who likes her drinks served in a coconut shell with a parasol attached." She laughed nervously. "Remember?"

"No coconut shells around here," he said, grabbing a bottle of Old Granddad and pouring himself two fingers. "So what's your pleasure?"

"Club soda." She cleared her throat. "Why don't you have some with me?"

"I'm happy with what I've got."

"I'm sure you are, but I don't think Dr. Ted would think it was such a great idea."

Lucky paused before answering, just long enough to make Martie uneasy. "So we won't tell Ted, will we, darlin'? Quality of life's just as important as quantity."

He reached for the bottle of club soda, filled a crystal tumbler, then handed it to her. Sunshine sparked off his gold wedding ring. She leaned forward to take the glass from him, feeling oddly off-balance. "I wish you could have been here for the party last night."

"So do I," he said. "Broke my heart, darlin'. Would've given anything to be there with you."

"So why didn't you?" she asked, a note of disappointment in her voice. "Obviously you're feeling better, or you wouldn't be here now."

"Little bit of engine trouble," he said. "Wanted to surprise you last night, but Tim said we needed to bring in a mechanic, and that took till morning."

"Tim didn't mention anything like that when I saw him."

"He come by the store?"

"I saw him at the airstrip. I was going to fly up to the ranch and talk to you."

Lucky laughed. "Estelle giving you trouble?"

"Estelle's always giving me trouble. That's nothing new." *Why are you hesitating? Tell him what's been going on. That's why you wanted to talk to him, isn't it?* She drew in a deep breath. "Did you happen to invite any old friends to the party, Daddy?"

"Old friends are the best friends," Lucky said. "I hope we had us a roomful of them."

She'd heard her father express those sentiments a thousand times before, yet this time they didn't sound quite right. That same prickling sense of unease danced up her spine, and this time it wouldn't be brushed away.

"There was somebody there who claimed to be an old friend of yours, but I don't think he was telling the truth."

Lucky took a swallow of bourbon. "Damn reporters," he said. "The vultures have been hovering since my heart gave out. Probably have me dead and buried."

"No, that wasn't it."

His expression didn't change, but his tension was unmistakable. "So what was it, darlin'? Someone from Tiffany, lookin' to rob us blind?"

She forced a smile. "I don't know his name, but he said he knew you from way back."

"That narrows it down to about ten thousand suspects."

"Any ideas?"

"Not without a name." He downed the rest of his drink. "How old a man was he?"

"Maybe thirty, thirty-five."

"I need more than that, girl."

"Tall, hazel eyes, not at all handsome, a curved scar on his left cheek—"

She gasped as Lucky pounced on her like a mountain lion. He grabbed her right forearm with his left hand.

"Where is he?" Lucky demanded, fingers digging into her soft skin with a pressure that bordered on cruelty.

"I don't know." She tried to pull away, but he held her fast.

"Don't lie to me, girl. Where is he?"

"I said I don't know!" His grip on her arm tightened, and she cried out.

Veins stood out at his temples and in his neck, and she was afraid he was courting another heart attack.

"When did you last see him?" he barked.

"A little while ago."

"An hour? A day? Five minutes?"

"I d-don't know," she stammered. "An hour... maybe two... I don't remember. What difference does it make? I—"

"Where did you see him? Did he come to the store? Here? Where?"

"Let go," she said, her voice taut with anger and fear. "You're hurting me."

He ignored her demand. "Damn it, girl, answer me. Where did you—?"

Her father's assistant appeared in the doorway, and Lucky released his hold on her arm. She watched, horrified, as a bland smile appeared on her father's face.

"Call for you, Mr. Wilde," the assistant said, with a pleasant nod in Martie's direction. "Line three. The gentleman says it's urgent."

"Be there directly," Lucky said, his smile steady.

His assistant nodded and left the room.

Lucky's smile vanished. "Stay put," he ordered Martie. "I'm not finished with you."

Her arm throbbed painfully as she paced the room, trying to make sense out of what had just happened. Like most successful men, Lucky could be arrogant and controlling and his temper often got the better of him, but he'd never been cruel, either physically or emotionally.

"Tonight," she heard her father say from the other room. "The plane is waiting, and we'd better..."

She tilted her head, listening. What was he talking about? The plane might be waiting, but the pilot wasn't. Tim had taken the little Cessna over to Galveston, and Lucky didn't know how to fly the jet. He'd believed he was too old and his reflexes too slow for him to safely pilot the powerful plane.

Lucky continued talking, but she couldn't make out all the words. He sounded angry and impatient, not at all like the loving, larger-than-life man who'd raised three little girls alone and done it well.

It was as if the father she knew and loved had been replaced by a total stranger.

A total stranger.

She froze, gripping the fragile back of a fan chair for support. She saw him as he'd reached for the bottle of Old Granddad, pouring the bourbon neatly with a twist of his left wrist. She saw the glint of sunlight on his golden wedding band as he'd handed her the glass of club soda.

Lucky was right-handed. He'd always said his left hand was about as useful as teats on a bull. Sweat broke out on her temples as an iron fist seemed to clamp down on her insides. She tried to push the foolish, dangerous thought from her mind, but it remained, growing stronger, more insistent, with each beat of her heart.

"Oh, God," she breathed, struggling beneath the weight of fear. The bourbon. His diminished body. The odd, almost covetous expression when she'd hugged him. Bile rose into her throat.

Your father's in danger. Help me get to him before it's too late.

Had the man been telling the truth?

She heard footsteps in the hallway. A late-afternoon breeze wafted through the open French doors. Quickly she slipped outside and ran toward the stand of live oaks that separated the main house from her cottage. She'd left her car at the end of the driveway, keys dangling from the ignition.

She slid behind the wheel. Her hands trembled as she started the engine. She threw the car into reverse and roared down the driveway in a wake of gravel. Loud voices came from the direction of the main house, along with the sounds of car doors slamming shut and auto engines leaping to life.

They want your father, and they won't give a damn if they have to kill you to get to him.

She refused to believe that the man responsible for the bruises on her arms was the man who'd dried her tears when she fell off her bicycle or beamed with pride when she went to her first formal dance.

She couldn't go to the police—not after last night. They already thought she was stark raving mad for claiming a man without fingerprints had broken into her home, tried to tie her to a chair, then rifled her lingerie drawer.

She'd seen the way the detectives exchanged knowing glances when the fingerprint report came back negative. If she called them again and said the man in her father's library wasn't her father at all, but a sadistic impersonator, they'd probably lock her up and throw away the key.

"Oh, God," she whispered as the reality of the situation slammed into her full-force. She didn't have a clue as to how to begin searching for Lucky. He could be two blocks away, or on the other side of the world.

Or he could be dead.

She refused to think about that. It wasn't even a possibility. It couldn't be. Lucky was her father. The man who'd raised her. They'd had their differences over the past ten years, but she'd never stopped loving him.

Help me find your father . . . he's in danger . . .

"Damn it to hell!" She pounded her fist on the steering wheel. She couldn't even turn to her sisters for help. Frankie was still in Hawaii, and Sam had left early that morning on a business trip to San Francisco.

"Think," she said out loud as she drove past the IMAX theater. Everyone knew there was no such thing as the perfect crime. Somehow, some way, even the cleverest criminals slipped up, and you didn't have to be Sherlock Holmes or Jessica Fletcher to add up the clues.

She was engrossed in thought, oblivious of everything, including the traffic light that had just turned red. If it hadn't been for a truck driver with a heavy hand on his horn, she might have plowed right through the white Porsche in front of her.

She slammed on the brakes, and the car screeched to a stop. Her arm shot over to keep her handbag from slipping off the seat, but she wasn't quick enough. It tumbled onto the rubber mat, and as she reached down to retrieve it, a spot of color caught her eye. A pack of matches with the words Yellow Rose Motel emblazoned diagonally across the cover in bold Day-Glo letters peeked out from under the seat.

She noted the address. Not exactly the best part of town. The Yellow Rose Motel was the kind of place you went to when you were too poor to stay someplace better.

Or when you wanted to stay anonymous?

She checked the glove compartment and silently thanked Lucky. Last year he'd said the day would come when she'd be glad she'd learned to use a gun. She'd just never figured it would be so soon.

She knew only one person who would stay in a place like the Yellow Rose.

Maybe it was time she paid him a surprise visit.

Chapter Eleven

The only reason Trask had come back to the room was to have one last crack at the color TV mounted on the Formica dresser. It was a cheap nineteen-inch model, the kind you'd find at Wal-Mart or some other discount store, but the few dollars he'd get from the pawnshop downtown could cover him until he managed to snag another credit card.

He'd been working at the damn thing for ten minutes with a metal nail file and a comb he'd found on the bathroom floor but so far no luck. If security at the White House was half as good as security at the Yellow Rose, the president would sleep better at night.

Muttering a curse, he flung the comb across the room. It bounced off the cheap standing lamp in the corner then fell to the floor. The TV wasn't going anywhere, and unless he got his butt moving, neither was he.

The pain in his rib was getting sharper, more insistent, and he knew what that meant. The countdown had begun. They'd homed in on him, and it was only a matter of hours until they found him, and once they found him, his problems would really start.

He tossed his few belongings into a duffel and zipped it closed, wishing he could do the same with his memories. They were with him when he opened his eyes each morning, and they haunted his dreams each night. They were so much a part of him that he hadn't even realized they were there until he held her in his arms at the country club and the years dropped away, filling him with a rush of hope and optimism he hadn't felt in longer than he could remember.

And she hadn't felt one damn thing.

She'd looked him straight in the eye, and she'd had no idea that the boy she'd loved was the man who stood before her. So much for his fantasies.

Yeah, she'd wanted him, but that was something different. Lust operated independently of the heart, and it was her heart he'd wanted. He'd had it once. She'd loved him with innocence and trust, and he'd felt as if he'd caught a glimpse of heaven right there on earth.

He should have known it couldn't last. Still, when he first saw her again after so many years, it had all come rushing back at him, a dizzying mix of love and desperation...and hope. There wasn't much in this life he hoped for, but in that moment he'd believed she would see through the years, through the changes, and understand.

She hadn't. She'd looked right through him, the way you'd look through a plate-glass window at the view outside. Hell, he knew he looked and sounded different—they'd seen to that—but somehow he'd believed she would know that what they'd shared, the dreams they'd dreamed, were still there waiting.

He cursed himself for a fool.

She had family and friends and a man who wanted to marry her and give her all the things he never could. He couldn't compete with that. He never could.

The wonder was that he'd even tried.

"BUY A VOWEL, girl," the desk clerk at the Yellow Rose muttered at the flickering screen as Martie stepped inside. "A *K?*" He met her eyes across the desk. "Don't take a whole lot of brains to know you don't waste your turn on a *K.*"

Martie, who had never seen "Wheel of Fortune" in her entire life, feigned enthusiasm. "That's right," she said, ignoring the Elvis calendar on the far wall and the Elvis clock behind the desk. "Everybody knows you should buy a *G.*"

The show broke for a commercial.

"You want a room?" the clerk asked.

She shook her head, horrified that he would ask such a thing. "I'm looking for someone."

The desk clerk kept one eye on the screen and one on Martie. "Ain't we all?"

She kept her hand in the pocket of her dress, fingers clenched around the barrel of the gun. "Maybe I should rephrase that. What I mean is, I'm looking for a *particular* person."

"You know his name?"

"No, I don't."

"So how'm I s'posed to help you find him?"

"He's tall, dark hair, a scar on his—" His expression flickered like the television screen. *Yes!* "He's here, isn't he?" She reached into her bag and withdrew a twenty-dollar bill. "What room is he in?"

"Twenty-one," said the clerk, pocketing the money while Vanna flipped over a letter, "but you didn't hear it from me."

The place was an utter cesspool of all manner of disgusting debris. She thought longingly of hip boots as she picked her way toward room 21, on the other side of the empty swimming pool. The murky, oily substance floating in it bore only a passing resemblance to water.

She shuddered and averted her eyes as she picked her way past broken beer bottles and cigarette butts. Televisions blared from behind closed doors: news reports and "Roseanne" reruns and MTV.

She didn't want to see him again. Every time she looked at him she found herself wanting things she had no business wanting. Certainly not from a man like that. He was driven by something dark and unknowable, and instinctively she knew she should turn and run, leap into her nice clean car and get as far away from here as she could.

But she knew she couldn't. Her father's life depended on it, and even if she was scared witless, even if she found herself tempted to risk everything, she had to see it through.

She stopped in front of room 21. It looked deserted. No sound squeaked through the door. No light leaked under the shabby green door. Faded curtains, the color of an old battleship, covered the sliding window, making it impossible for her to peer inside.

There was no reason to think he was in there, but she sensed his presence, like a vibration deep inside her bones, and that fact scared her more than any other danger she might face.

TRASK WAS halfway to the door when someone knocked. Actually, *pounded* was more like it. He stopped, senses on red alert, then remembered that the people he was running from didn't bother to announce their arrival.

"Ten seconds," said a familiar voice. "If you don't open that door, so help me, I'll—"

He dropped the duffel and swung the door open. Martie stood there on his doorstep, looking angrier and more dangerous than she had a few hours ago, which was fine with him, since he was feeling more than a little angry and dangerous himself.

"What the hell are you doing here?" he asked in lieu of greeting.

"You might want to ask what I'm doing here with a *gun.*"

Damn. He hadn't noticed the gun. It was there, all right, pointing straight between his eyes. He had no doubt Lucky's daughter would be a good shot. A few scenarios presented themselves, all of which had to do with the spilling of blood, and none of them were pleasant.

"That thing isn't loaded, is it?"

"Don't insult my intelligence."

"Is that a yes or a no?"

"Want to try your luck?" she countered.

He didn't. The way things had been going lately, he'd end up buried behind the motel swimming pool.

Martie pushed past him into the motel room, keeping the gun trained on the furrow in his brow. "I need your help."

He laughed out loud. "That's one hell of a way to ask for it."

"Believe me, I don't want to ask you for any-thing, but you're my last chance." She swallowed hard. "Damn it, I don't know why, but I trust you."

"Right," he said dryly. "That's why you have a gun pointed at my head. Should I feel flattered?"

"I don't give a damn," she snapped. Her hand was shaking. He hoped her trigger finger wasn't. "The only thing I care about is finding my fa-ther."

He moved toward the center of the room. Even a good shot might have trouble with a moving tar-get. "I thought I was the one who couldn't find your father."

"I'm not in the mood for jokes," she said, her words taut and angry, despite her obvious anxiety. "You've said things—lots of things. That Lucky is in danger, that you needed to find him before it's too late. What did you mean by that? What kind of danger? Tell me," she demanded, her voice rising. *"Tell me!"*

"Put the gun down and we'll talk."

"Talk first, then I'll put the gun down."

Even Trask had to admit his bargaining power was limited. The only thing he had on his side was the element of surprise. Moving swiftly, he slammed the door shut and threw the latch.

"Okay," he said, moving closer to her. "Let's talk."

This wasn't what Martie had expected. Alone in that motel room, he seemed bigger than she remembered, and a great deal more dangerous. The crescent-shaped scar on his cheek took on an ominous dimension in the tiny room. Fear lodged at the base of her throat.

"You talk tough for a girl." He bellied up to the barrel of the gun. "You don't have the guts to pull the trigger."

"Don't push me," she warned. "I protect my own. If you don't tell me what's going on, so help me, I'll blast you back to wherever you came from."

"I'm on your side, Princess," he said, not backing down. "I always have been."

The words resonated in the air between them, and she found herself struck by a sense of inevitability, of destiny.

He's a liar and a thief, Martie. Don't let him con you into believing anything else.

But the emotions swelling behind her breastbone were so strong that she found herself wavering suddenly between resolve and surrender. His eyes, she thought as she looked at him over the barrel of her gun.

Those sad hazel eyes looked at her from that ravaged face, and they were her undoing. In those eyes, she saw anger and pain, and a sadness so deep and wide she feared her heart would break of it.

And she also saw something else, something hauntingly familiar that danced just beyond reach...

She raised her left arm to push her hair from her face, and her sleeve slipped down.

"What the hell is that?" He gestured toward the angry purple bruises on her forearm.

She lowered her arm and let the sleeve drop back into place. "I'd tell you it was a little gift from my father, except I refuse to believe that the man who did it is Lucky."

That someone would touch her like that, that someone would even think about it, was obscene.

He held out his hands to her, oblivious of the gun and her anger, oblivious of everything but what they'd once shared. She was afraid of him, and she probably had reason to be. He was no damn good for her, never had been any good for her, right from the start.

"Give me your hands."

"No."

"Your hands."

"Go to hell."

"I can help you."

Her eyes filled with tears. "If you want to help me, help me find Lucky, tell me he isn't—"

"I can't."

"Damn you," she whispered, glancing away. "*Damn* you."

She was vulnerable, and he used that vulnerability to his advantage, taking the gun from her with only a brief struggle. He jammed it into the waistband of his jeans, then took her hands in his.

"Don't," she said, misreading his intentions. "I don't want this."

"Trust me, Martie. Just one more time . . ."

One more time. The words echoed inside her head. What did he mean, one more time? She'd first met him less than twenty-four hours ago. It wasn't like they shared a history of any kind.

He moved his hands up over her wrists to her forearms, and she gasped when he placed his palms over the ugly bruises with a firm pressure. The pain shot all the way up to her shoulders.

"Relax," he said, in that rough-honey voice. "Trust me."

"No," she said, starting to pull away. "I don't want to trust you."

"A minute ago you said you trusted me."

"For answers."

"I can help you."

"Do what?" she asked on a nervous laugh, as the pressure increased. "You're hurting me."

"It won't last."

"Let me go," she said. His intensity was beginning to frighten her.

A charge of electricity shot through Trask, a pleasant tingle at first, a little jolt of current, but quickly it grew more intense, the sensations coming faster and faster, harder and harder, until he felt as if his forearms had been pummeled with a sledgehammer.

He'd done this before. He knew how it should feel. Something was wrong. He opened his eyes against the waves of red-hot pain washing over him and looked at her. Instead of smiling up at him, she looked on the verge of passing out. Her face was drained of color, and sweat beaded her brow.

He was hurting her. Damn it, the pain was supposed to be his. He welcomed her pain, needed it to banish the demons, but it wasn't working. Instead of obliterating her pain, he was multiplying it. Her breathing was shallow, her pulse rapid. She was spinning backward into the darkness, spinning out of his reach, spinning away from him forever.

Were they close enough to have activated the reversal process that was the key to their plans? At the touch of a button, his healing gift could be transformed into something deadly.

The perfect murder, they called it. As swift and sure as a bullet to the brain, but without the ugliness.

Without the evidence.

And it was going to happen right here, right now, unless he could find a way to stop it before the only woman he'd ever loved became the first person he killed.

Chapter Twelve

Nerve-shattering bursts of electrical energy curled Martie's fingers into fists as the pain pulsed its way up her arms and into her chest. Her heart felt as if it were being squeezed in a drill press, while her lungs struggled for each breath.

She tried to pull away, but he held her fast. "Stop!" she cried as the pain grew stronger. "Please—" *I'm going to die,* she thought. *He's trying to kill me....*

"Trying to..." he managed, each word obviously spoken with great difficulty. "Didn't want to hurt you..."

Trying to? What did he mean—he was *trying* to stop? They weren't tied together in any way. His hands weren't clamped to her forearm. All he had to do was let go.

But he didn't. Or he couldn't. It was hard for her to think clearly over the waves of pain. It seemed as if he were trying to release her, but maybe he was just a brilliant criminal.

The muscles in his shoulders and chest strained as he struggled to break the connection between them. A silver chain hung from his neck, and a chunky medal of unpolished silver swung hypnotically with every move he made.

She looked more closely. It wasn't a medal at all, it was a ring. Her stomach knotted. A heavy ring of unpolished silver with a deep blue stone sunk deep in the center of it.

She knew that ring. The memory of how it had felt beneath her fingers as she fashioned it from a nugget of metal lingered, despite the years. She'd made it for Trask the night they met, molding the silver into a shape that was as bold and strong as the man who watched her, his hazel eyes intent upon her every move. She'd felt powerful, and utterly female, as if she could bend their future to her design, the same way she could bend the precious metal. But they hadn't had a future at all, had they? Their future had vanished in a heartbeat, leaving her alone. She began to tremble. Where had this man found the ring? It couldn't— No, things like this didn't happen, not in the real world. She'd given up believing in miracles a long time ago. Things like this didn't happen, not in the real world.

There'd been an auto accident out near the airport. She could still see the sadness in her father's eyes as he'd broken the terrible news to her. Her father wouldn't have lied to her... not about something like that. Not about someone's life.

She looked again at the man before her. His eyes... those sad and beautiful hazel eyes. For a moment, the world vanished and she was seventeen again and in love for the first and only time in her life.

Trask, she thought, her heart beating fast and hard. This man didn't look or sound or act like the man she'd loved, but the sudden towering joy that filled her heart couldn't be denied.

A thousand memories came back at her in a violent rush, piling one on top of the other so fast and so hard that she couldn't breathe or think or do anything but whisper his name over and over again, knowing it was impossible.

"Trask."

He couldn't remember the last time he'd heard someone speak his name. They'd taken everything from him, his face, his voice, his past. Hearing her say his name was a balm to his spirit, and he could feel strength filling his body where moments ago there'd been nothing but pain.

He reached down deep into his soul, past the loneliness and the anger and the regret, and found a miracle. With a strength born of desperation and love, he pushed her away from him and sagged to the ground. The gun fell from his waistband and rolled under the plastic coffee table.

She knelt down next to him, the scent of jasmine surrounding him. If she realized her bruises were gone, she gave no indication of it. She reached out and touched the ring.

"Wh-where did you get this?"

For the first time, the easy lie eluded him.

She leaned closer, her beautiful aqua eyes level with his. "I asked you a question—where did you get this ring?"

He couldn't run away from it. Not any longer. "You know where I got it, Martie."

"You stole this from someone, didn't you, or maybe you found it in a pawn shop and—" Her voice cracked, and she swallowed hard. "Oh, God," she whispered as her eyes filled with tears. "It's true—"

"I didn't want it to be this way," he said, his voice hoarse with emotion. "I—"

Her hand cracked against his jaw with the force of ten years of loss and anger. "You son of a bitch! When were you planning to tell me who you are?"

His face hurt like hell, and he was glad. It was less than he deserved. "I wasn't planning on it."

Her body jerked as if she'd been struck. "Blunt, aren't you?"

"You deserved the truth."

"Oh, yes," she said as tears mingled with bitter laughter. "I deserve the truth. How kind of you to consider my feelings."

It was like walking into the eye of a storm, but he'd gone too far to run for shelter now. "I didn't come back to hurt you. I didn't want it to be this way."

"You were going to wait for me to guess who you are?" Her voice was deadly calm. She wondered how it was possible, when she felt as if she were standing in the center of a whirlwind. She rose to her feet and stood over him, consumed by a rage so powerful it threatened to break free and destroy them both. "Were you going to see how long it took the fool to figure it all out?"

"You weren't supposed to figure it out," he said, as he stood to face her. "You were supposed to take me to your father."

"And never realize that you were—"

"That's right. You weren't supposed to know."

"Are you telling me my father is in on this, too, that the two of you cooked up this whole disgusting little scheme together?"

"No, that's not what I'm telling you. I've been trying to find your father for weeks. He doesn't know I'm in town."

"But he knows you're alive," she said prodding. "He doesn't think you're dead, or anything ridiculous like that."

"He knows I'm alive," he shot back. "What the hell does that have to do with anything?"

She grabbed for her gun, which had rolled under the plastic coffee table, then pointed it at him. "So tell me how it is, Trask Benedict. Why don't you tell me how much fun you had making a fool out of me?"

A bullet whizzed past his left shoulder.

"What the hell did you do that for?"

"I wish you were dead," she cried, the gun hanging loosely from her hand as the acrid smell of gunpowder filled the room. "I'd finally made my peace with it... I was finally able to accept the fact that you were gone, and I was ready to get on with my life. Now you're back, and—"

The gun clattered to the carpet. Neither of them noticed. Heaven was in that room.

Their gazes locked.

Their hearts cracked open.

They came together in anger and heat, a fierce mating that was part celebration, part battle.

"Oh, God..." That couldn't be her voice, that mournful, triumphant, keening sound.

A deep moan tore from his throat, more powerful than words.

He ravished her mouth with his, drawing the breath from her body and making it his while her hungry, eager hands tore at his clothes, stripping him of everything but his aching, throbbing need for her.

And it was for her. All of it. Every powerful inch. She bent down to take him in her mouth, and he almost exploded at the first touch of her lips against his heated, swollen flesh. He pulled her up the length of his body, reaching under her dress to tear off the scrap of lace, then cupped her buttocks in his hands while she wrapped her legs around his hips.

He didn't ask if she was ready.

She didn't ask him to be gentle.

They were beyond that. The hunger between them was too great. With a primal cry of possession, he lowered her onto his powerful erection, then sank into her soft and willing body.

She cried out when he entered her, but it was a cry of conquest. She felt herself opening wide, then wider still, to accommodate his size, felt dark ripples of sensation that seemed to start deep inside her womb and move outward.

Her body hugged his, her muscles contracting around his shaft, driving him higher and higher, until he exploded inside her.

She caught his fire and shuddered, then came in a shattering climax that left her spent and crying against his shoulder.

Together they fell to the battered sofa in that ugly room and found the beauty and joy that had eluded them for so very long.

It was everything Trask had needed, but nothing he'd wanted. From the moment he saw her in line in the supermarket, he'd known it was going to end like this, known that all the defenses he'd constructed, year by painful, lonely year, would come tumbling down around him, leaving him vulnerable in a way he'd thought he would never be vulnerable again.

It was a terrible thing for a man like Trask Benedict to love someone. Loving made you want things you couldn't have, things that other people took for granted, like air and food and water. It had been easier when his life had no meaning, when he walked through the days on automatic pilot, when he didn't feel this fierce, desperate joy in being alive, in being here at this moment, with this woman naked and satisfied in his arms.

For Martie, it was like waking up from a terrible dream of darkness and loss to find the sun shining...to find that she was no longer alone. She loved him with the same elemental force that kept her heart beating. It was so much a part of her, so basic and necessary, that it required no thought, no effort. He was a part of her soul. Even when she believed him dead, she had continued to love him.

Some might have called it madness, to love so deeply and so well, when there was no hope of seeing that love returned, but she'd never had a choice in the matter. From the very start, from the moment the world was created, they'd been destined to be together.

She cupped his ravaged face between her hands as sorrow washed over her. "What happened?" she whispered. "Who did this to you?"

"It's been a rough life," he said. "Things happen. People change."

"You don't even sound the same."

He said nothing.

She felt like crying for what he'd lost, what they'd lost. She'd loved his beauty, and she mourned its passing, but it had only been part of what had bound her to him. The connection went deeper, ran truer, than that.

"I dreamed of this so many times," she murmured against his mouth. "Sometimes late at night, when I couldn't sleep, I would remember how you smelled, the sound of your voice."

"You were supposed to forget me." He sounded old and terribly sad. Why didn't he sound as joyous and blessed as she felt? "Get on with your life."

"I couldn't. A crazy part of me always believed we still had a chance."

"We don't stand a chance in hell," he said, pushing her away. "We never did. This shouldn't have happened."

"Oh, God." Her heart jumped up into her throat. "You're married." Her voice was low, little more than a whisper. A wife and kids and a home in the country, complete with a white picket fence. All the things she'd thought they would have together.

"No," he said, a faint smile tilting his mouth. "I'm not married." He grasped her hips and rolled her over on top of him. "But you've got yourself a fiancé back home."

She slipped off the seven-carat ring and tossed it across the room. "Not anymore."

"You don't want to lose that, Princess. Old Jason's the better bet."

"No," she said, laying her fingertips against the angry scar on his cheek. "There's only you. Right from the start, there was only you."

"It's been a long time," he said, thinking of the empty years they'd lost, the things he had done to fill the hours. "There must have been someone."

She shook her head. "It drove Lucky crazy. That's why he finally came up with his ultimatum."

"Ultimatum?"

"Marry or else," she said. How silly it all sounded now, as she lay in the arms of the only man she'd ever loved. "Lucky came up with the idea after his heart attack. Sam and Frankie said they'd rather sling hash somewhere than marry someone they didn't love, but the work was all I had. It is—it was—everything to me. If I lost that . . ."

And he heard what she couldn't say. That she'd been so lonely for so long that even a loveless marriage based on nothing but convenience was better than growing old with no one and nothing to call her own.

"Why did you leave?" she whispered, feeling the pain as if it were new. "Did he give you money? Did he threaten you? I have to know."

"It's over," he said. "It doesn't matter anymore."

"It matters," she said fiercely. "I loved you. I thought you loved me." An odd coldness came into her eyes, a coldness he felt in his own heart. "Or was I just a foolish little rich girl who was ripe for the taking?"

"It wasn't like that," he said. "I left because it was better that way." Because it was the only way he could help Lucky to keep danger away from her.

"Better for who?" she demanded. "Better for my father? Better for your bank account? Better for Lucky?"

"What about Lucky?" he countered. "You came here to tell me something—"

"I don't give a damn about Lucky." Her voice was suddenly cold. "He can go to hell." He'd played God with their lives for ten years. She'd never give him another chance. Not ever.

"You don't mean that."

"The hell I don't."

"He's your father."

"In name only. Sam and Frankie are his blood. I'm the stranger in the family. Maybe I finally realized it."

"He loves you, Martie."

"He loves himself," she snapped, "and he loves power and influence and playing God."

"You've got it wrong."

"Look at you!" she cried. "You have nothing! Look at this place! I saw you hanging around the cash machine at Fiesta. I'm not a stupid woman, Trask. I know why you were there."

He didn't deny it.

"Don't you see?" she continued. "It would've been different if we'd stayed together. You could have made something of yourself. You wouldn't have ended up stealing credit cards to get by."

"You don't know what you're saying."

"Lucky should have died," she said, unable to hide her bitterness. "The heart attack should have finished him off. It's what he deserved." She stopped. "I must have been crazy to think some impostor had taken Lucky's place. That was him, all right. I just never realized what a total bastard he is. Finally, his true colors—''

Trask went on red alert. "An impostor?"

"The bruises on my arms," she said, rolling up her sleeves. "Lucky grabbed me when I mentioned you, and I guess my imagination got the better of me." She stopped. Strange, but her arms didn't hurt any longer. The pain was totally, completely gone, as if it had never been there in the first place, and, to her shock, her skin was unmarred. "You did this, didn't you? This is what you were doing to me!"

"Guilty."

The breath left her body in an audible *whoosh*. "H-how?"

"I don't know."

"You must know."

He shrugged. "I put my hands on you, I hurt like hell, you felt better. Pretty simple."

"You've done this kind of thing before?"

"A few times."

Her knees buckled, and she sank to the floor. "What other secrets are you keeping from me? Next thing I know, you'll be telling me you're a superspy with secret powers."

"I *am* a spy."

"Sure," said Martie. "And I suppose Lucky's a spy, too."

"Yes."

She waited for the punch line. "That's it?" she said. "Hello, how are you, I'm a spy? Lies need a little embellishment, Trask, if they're going to be believable."

He lifted his T-shirt and pointed toward a quarter-inch scar beneath one of his ribs. It had been pulsing like a son of a bitch in there. He wouldn't be surprised if she saw his skin ripple. "There's a microchip in there."

"A 486 or a Pentium?" She looked torn between annoyance and laughter. "I think you can do better than this, Trask. Sounds like you've been watching too much James Bond, if you ask me."

"This isn't James Bond," he snapped, crouching down in front of her, forcing her to meet his eyes. "This is real."

"You're joking, right?" Her voice quavered just enough for him to notice. "They did this in *Jaws,* didn't they, throw in a few jokes just before the great white leaps onto the boat and has them for breakfast."

"Lucky has enemies," he said, "powerful enemies, and they'll stop at nothing to destroy him."

"Enemies? What do you mean, like Tiffany or Cartier?"

"Yeah," he said, exasperated. "Jewelers are real tough."

"Lucky doesn't have enemies. He has competitors, but he doesn't have enemies." Everyone loved her father. Everyone but Martie.

"You were right—the man at the house isn't your father." Lucky had entrée to so many important, and reclusive figures on the world scene that it had only been a matter of time before they substituted one of their own for the Texas jeweler. Trask was only surprised that they hadn't done it sooner.

"No," she said, backpedaling. "I know I said that—"

"Your instincts were dead-on. They've got your father, and I think I know where he is."

"They? Who is *they*? The Girl Scouts? The CIA? The KGB?"

"You're getting close." And so were they. He felt as if he had a mongoose swinging from his rib.

She swung out with her fist and clipped him in the thigh. "Damn it, if this is your idea of a joke—"

"Put your clothes on."

She looked up at him. *"What?"*

"Get dressed. We're getting out of here." He'd given it his best shot. Now they were out of time.

"I'm not going anywhere until I get some answers."

"You're going to have to trust me on this one."

"Trust you?" Martie looked up at him, her eyes wide. "You pop up again ten years after I thought you died, tell me that my father is missing, that someone else has taken his place, and that you're a superspy with a microchip planted in your belly, and you expect me to just sit back and trust you? Call me suspicious, but I'm afraid I need a little more explanation than 'Trust me.'"

"Where are you going to go?" he reasoned, aware of how quickly the minutes were passing. "You can't go back to the house. Hell, you can't stay in Houston, not until we know what's going on. I'm your best bet, Princess. Hell, the way I see it, I'm your only bet."

"I'll go to the police," she said, even though she knew how absurd an idea that was. "I'll call the FBI. There has to be someone who can help—"

Her jaw dropped open in surprise. He had her gun, and it was pointing straight at her. "I'm not asking you, Princess, I'm telling you, and since you weren't shy about pulling the trigger, you can damn well bet I won't be, either. Move it *now*."

Chapter Thirteen

St. Brendan's, an island off the coast of Scotland

"It always comes down to this," Lucky Wilde said as the slender, dark-eyed man walked into the drafty room, followed by a phalanx of goons. "Two bitter old men deciding the fate of the young ones." As with war, there was something obscene about it.

Viktor had always fancied himself a cut above the common throng. He dismissed his bodyguards with an imperious wave of his hand and turned to Lucky. "You sound petulant, old friend. You should be gracious in defeat. The battle was engaged, and I emerged victorious."

Lucky fought the urge to spit at the man's feet. Defeat? The hell it was. This was his show from beginning to end, even if the son of a bitch standing before him didn't realize it. He'd been working toward this moment ever since his phony heart attack. All the months of planning, calculating, bullying, in order to get to this point.

It was a given that he wouldn't leave this ramshackle castle alive, but this was his chance to ensure that Martie and his other daughters had the futures they deserved.

And the key to it all was the slender man in the fancy suit who stood before him.

Lucky was at a disadvantage right now but that wouldn't last. They weren't the only ones who knew how to manipulate that little microchip beneath an operative's rib cage. Lucky had more than a few tricks up his sleeve too. With a few modifications, PAX had managed to create a twenty-first-century communications device that could be activated by a single password, summoning a SWAT team that could take down a dictator, topple a government, or just save a few innocent lives. Before the day was over the pendulum would swing in Lucky's direction, and Viktor would finally know how it felt to be vulnerable.

To know you were going to die, and that there wasn't a damn thing you could do to stop it.

The way his wife had felt when Viktor wrapped those slender hands and squeezed the life from her while their baby daughter slept in the other room.

I owe you, Lucky thought, his expression as bland as he could manage. *And today the debt will be paid.*

"I would raise a toast to you, Viktor, but my hands are otherwise occupied." They'd tied him to a high-backed chair, both hands and feet. It flattered the hell out of him that they thought he was still that dangerous. They didn't know the half of it.

Viktor's full lips pulled back in a smile. "I trust you are not terribly uncomfortable."

"I'll live," Lucky drawled. Maybe not for long, but that was another story.

"Tonight we will have the chance to settle old issues between us."

"We could've talked in Houston," Lucky observed.

"Perhaps yes," said Viktor, "but the facilities on this side of the Atlantic are far superior to anything your country has yet to offer, for what we have in mind."

You fell for it, hook, line and sinker, Viktor. He blessed predictability.

"Don't suppose we're talkin' food now, are we?" Lucky asked.

"Always the joke with you, old friend. Tonight, however, is special—we are expecting a guest."

Viktor's smile sharpened, and Lucky felt the sting of its blade. "Tonight we welcome my daughter Martina."

MARTIE maintained a stony face on their way to the airstrip as Trask outlined his plan.

"I resent this," she said. "You had no right to take my gun."

"You're lucky I didn't use it on you," he said. "You weren't this stubborn ten years ago."

"I wasn't a woman ten years ago," she shot back, "I was a girl. You can't pop up out of nowhere and take over my life, Trask. I won't allow it." *No matter how much I love you.*

"I had to get your attention," he said.

"Guns will do that."

"If it makes you feel better, Princess, this is my first kidnapping."

"Wonderful," she drawled. "That really makes my day."

"If we can get the jet, we have a chance," he said as he swung the stolen rental car onto a side street. "If not, we'll have to come up with something else and fast. The longer they have Lucky, the tougher this is going to be."

"We can't use the jet," she said, breaking her self-imposed silence. "Daddy's pilot has gone home to see his new grandbaby. There's no one to fly the plane."

"I'll do it."

"You can fly?"

He nodded.

"A *jet?*"

"Lucky taught me."

She leaned back in her seat and crossed her arms over her chest. "Of course you can fly a jet. You're a superspy." The word dripped with sarcasm. "And I suppose you speak French, German, and Greek fluently, read Sanskrit, and maintain a small army for your personal amusement."

"You don't believe me."

Her eyes widened. "Whatever gave you that idea?"

He supposed he couldn't blame her for not believing him. It did sound pretty fantastic.

"So let's pretend you really can fly a jet," she said, baiting him. "Where would you plan on flying it to?"

"You'll find out when we get there."

"No answer, no plane."

"No plane, no father." He looked at her. "It's my ball game now, Princess."

"What if the plane's not there?" she said after another few moments passed. "My sister Sam might've had it flown to New York to bring her home." The fact that Sam was way too frugal to do something that frivolous was beside the point.

"Then we'll charter a flight." He flipped down the sun visor against the Texas glare. "Hope you brought plastic."

Her jaw locked with anger, and they didn't speak again until they reached the airstrip. The purples and blues of twilight were deepening as lights began to dot the landscape. A tiny Cessna taxied into position for takeoff as they swung into a parking spot, and seconds later it raced down the runway and lifted into the air.

Trask reached into his duffel and withdrew some impressive-looking papers. "My name is Royce Canfield," he said in a low voice that brooked no argument. "I was an air force pilot. I flew for eight years with Pan Am, and when they went under, I went corporate."

She looked down at the license and passport. "Where did you get this?"

"You can get just about anything, if you know where to look."

"Including illegal documents?"

He hated the fear and uncertainty in her beautiful eyes, but there was no help or it. Not right now. The mongoose clinging to his rib cage had turned into a barracuda. He glanced at his watch. A little after eight. If his calculations were right, they had no more than twenty minutes to get airborne before his pursuers pinpointed his latitude and longitude to the precise degree.

Fortunately, Lucky believed in keeping his planes ready for action at all times. Fifteen minutes after they arrived, Martie was seated next to Trask in the cockpit, seat belt fastened, fingernails gripping the armrest.

She'd been sure someone would question Trask about the pilot's license or make a phone call to check up on him, but the moment the controller noticed Martie waiting for Trask, he'd just smiled and waved them through.

"You're carrying the joke a little far, don't you think?" she asked as they took their seats in the cockpit.

He glanced at her, then slipped on the headphones and began to do strange things with the myriad dials and buttons on the instrument panel.

"I could do that, too," she said. "That doesn't mean you know what you're doing."

She had a moment's hesitation when the engines roared to life, and a second of major apprehension when the ground crew cleared them to taxi over to the runway, but she honestly expected him to finally admit he'd been bluffing.

Reality hit her full force when they barreled down the runway and took off.

Trask glanced at her as they gained altitude. "I won't say I told you so."

"Thank you," she managed.

A few hours later they landed at a small airfield in Teterboro, in northern New Jersey.

"New Jersey?" she asked with a lift of her brow, as the plane rolled past the Welcome to Teterboro sign and came to a stop.

"We need to refuel."

"Refuel? The only thing east of New Jersey is the Atlantic Ocean, and—" She stopped and stared at him. "Where are you taking me?"

"We'll talk when I come back," he said, unbuckling his seat belt and standing up. "This won't take long."

She watched as he exited the plane then spent a few moments talking to the ground crew. *You can make a run for it, Martie. Unbuckle the belt, stand up, and run for your life.* She had money with her, and credit cards. She even had her driver's license and passport. Everything a nineties woman needed to make an escape.

So why didn't she?

You've lost what's left of your mind. For all you know, he killed Lucky and he's taking you hostage.

She was the daughter of a very wealthy man. The same man who'd said Trask wasn't good enough to marry her. What if he'd been nursing a ten-year grudge, and now it was time to get his revenge?

But there it was again, the bone-deep, soul-shattering certainty that, no matter how strange or frightening or unbelievable the situation might be, she was where she was meant to be.

The first time she'd felt this way, she'd been seventeen years old, naive and eager to believe in love. She wasn't seventeen any longer, and she certainly wasn't naive. She'd thought her belief in love had died along with Trask, but tonight—miraculously—both had come back to her, and she wasn't about to let them go.

Thirty minutes later, Trask reboarded the jet and took his seat next to Martie. He slipped on the headphones and tried to forget how much he wanted to touch the soft skin of her cheek, her silky hair, her—

No point going down that particular path. They had a long flight ahead of them, and he needed to stay sharp. He started the engine, then taxied out to the start of the runway. Moments later, they were once again airborne.

And that was when she nailed him.

"I want to know what the hell is going on," she said in a deadly calm voice. "Don't patronize me. Don't try to protect me. Don't do one damn thing except tell me the truth. If you can't do that, then there's no hope for us, and we may as well know that right now."

He looked into her eyes, and he saw the girl he'd fallen in love with all those years ago, and it damn near broke his heart to think they didn't stand a chance. He loved her. The depth of emotion inside his heart shattered the last of his illusions. This wasn't just about saving his own butt any longer, it wasn't about saving the world. It was about this woman.

He thought about how much easier it would be if he didn't give a damn about her, if she'd been nothing more than an easy lay, a quick roll down memory lane. But she wasn't. She was his past. She was his present. And if things had been different, he knew she would have been his future. Silently he cursed the Fates that had brought her back into his life when the odds were stacked against him and his time was running out.

Maybe he couldn't give her forever, but he could give her the truth as he knew it.

"I met Lucky in Budapest," he said as the jet climbed above the clouds. "Eleven years ago..."

St. Brendan's Island

MARTIE WAS EN ROUTE to the castle.

Lucky didn't want to believe it, but the gleam in Viktor's eyes told him it was true.

What kind of trap had he set for his own daughter, the child of his heart? Despair unlike anything he'd ever known tore at his heart.

"She does not know about me?" Viktor asked as Lucky finished the last of his dinner. They had untied his hands long enough for him to eat, something he found ironic, given the circumstances.

"She knows she's adopted," Lucky said, wishing the Riesling was a Lone Star. Wishing he was back in Texas.

"But she knows nothing of her parentage?"

"She knows I'm her father."

"You are not her father. It is my blood that runs through her veins."

Lucky took the glass of wine and threw it against the stone wall behind Viktor's head. "You can have whatever you want, you sadistic son of a bitch, but leave my daughter alone."

Viktor glanced at his watch. A feral smile creased his face. He reminded Lucky of a rabid coyote. "They are running late," he said in his precise English. "I estimate they will be here within the hour."

Lucky didn't bother to fight the bold statement. There wasn't much that PAX, or its offshoot, couldn't make happen when it put its mind to it. "Tim isn't much for flyin' into strange places. He'll have himself one hell of a fight with that sad little airstrip you scraped out back there." He prayed Tim hit foul weather or a minor mechanical problem. Anything to ground him far away from St. Brendan's.

"Ah, yes," said Viktor, "I knew there was one thing I had neglected to tell you. Martina will be accompanied by her lover."

If he'd been thirty years younger, Lucky would have leapt to his feet and shoved Viktor's teeth down his wrinkled throat, cap by cap. "Martie and Jason are engaged to be married. Whatever they do or don't do sure ain't any of your damn business." He'd come up with the entire marry-or-else scheme to ensure his daughters' happiness once he was gone.

"Jason Blackburn?" Viktor's aristocratic brow creased in puzzlement. "There is much you do not know, old friend. Martina isn't traveling with Jason Blackburn. She is traveling with an old compatriot of yours."

Oh, God, thought Lucky. The web of intrigue spread even farther than he'd feared. Who the hell else had gone over to the other side?

"Bryan Grant?" he asked.

"Grant?" Viktor spat the man's name as if it were a piece of spoiled meat. "The man I speak of is much more important to you, Lucky Wilde. You nurtured him, you took him under your considerable—how you say?—wing, and he repaid your largesse by stealing Martina's virtue. Trask Benedict hasn't been heard from much lately, but we have plans to change that."

"Sloppy fact-finding," Lucky said, as the cold hand of fear gripped him by the throat. "Take another look at your files, Viktor. Trask died two years ago."

"How little you know, old friend."

"Five shots at close range."

"He lives."

"I have the termination notice in my safe. He was thirty-four."

"He is thirty-six now."

"You're lying."

"I have no need of lies, when the truth is so delicious."

"He would have gotten in touch with me." Every year or two, an encrypted message from Trask had found its way to Lucky's desk, and each time Lucky's answer had been the same: *She lives*.

"He has been trying to."

No, Lucky thought, the pain in his chest radiating wider. "You're a lying son of a bitch."

"I am a son of a bitch," Viktor conceded, "but I am not lying. He was at Martina's party, and..."

"No—"

"...he was looking for you..."

"God, no!"

"...but he found Martina again, and the rest, as you say, is history."

Everything Lucky had feared, every cold-sweat-down-the-back-of-your-neck nightmare he'd ever had, was about to come true, and there wasn't one damn thing he could do to stop it.

Chapter Fourteen

Martie's eyes were wide in the darkened cabin. "You stole Lucky's wallet?"

"I gave it my best shot, but your old man was a lot faster than he looked." He told her of Lucky's connection to his parents and of the way her father had taken Trask under his wing and introduced him to PAX.

"You love him, don't you?" she asked, remembering his reaction when she'd first mentioned Lucky's heart attack.

He looked straight ahead. "He's the father I never had." Trask's own father had raised him, but he'd never been there for Trask. He hadn't realized he'd been looking for guidance until he met Lucky Wilde.

"You're telling me that my father, the man I've known since almost the day I was born, is really a spy?"

"He's been a spy since the start of the Korean War."

She sank back down into her seat. "Lucky's been a spy for forty-five years?"

"And a damn good one."

"How long have you been a spy?" Just saying it made her want to laugh out loud. James Bond was a spy. Boris and Natasha were spies. But Lucky and Trask? Impossible.

"Almost eleven years," he said.

"That's it, isn't it?" she asked. "That's why he wanted to break us up."

"He worried about you and your sisters. The last thing he wanted was for you to get hooked up with an operative."

"He married and raised a family," she pointed out, unable to keep the anger from her voice. "Why was it different for me?"

"It's not a good life, Princess."

"I can see that," she said, gesturing toward his worn clothes and battered duffel. But it wouldn't have mattered to her. They could have found a way to make it work between them.

He was glad she'd misunderstood. He sure as hell didn't want to be the one to tell her that her mother had been murdered by her father's archenemy, the notorious Viktor.

She gestured toward his face. "Is that how..." Her words trailed off. She was embarrassed to have even brought up the subject.

"I was shot," he said without embarrassment. "I died two years ago, on the deck of a ship in the South China Sea. A PAX operative was on board, and somehow managed to save my ass. Too bad he'd already shifted allegiance to the other side."

"Wait," she said, holding up her hand. "You died?"

"I flatlined for almost three minutes, and somehow they managed to get back a pulse and take me to a hospital."

"That still doesn't explain the way you look or sound or—"

"After my condition stabilized, they shipped me off to a private hospital in Switzerland, and that's where the fun started."

"Plastic surgery?"

"State-of-the-art. New face, new voice, new DNA. I couldn't prove my existence to my own mother, if she were still alive." He held out one hand, palm outward. "No fingerprints. Check it out."

She started to laugh, in spite of herself. "How I wish I could get you to show that to the Houston Police Department."

"It wasn't all bad," he said. "That's where the healing thing started—or at least where I found out about it." One of the nurses had spilled hot coffee on her leg, and he'd reached out to steady her, and they'd both watched in amazement as the pain, the blistering and the coffee stain all disappeared.

"My panty hose," she said, remembering. "You made a run disappear the night of my engagement party."

"That was last night," he reminded her.

She shook her head in bemusement. "It seems like another lifetime."

A bump of turbulence rocked the plane, and they were quiet for the moments it took to find the groove again.

"There's something I still don't understand," she continued. "You were already working under-cover. Had you compromised the organization in some way? Why would they do this to you?"

"PAX lost its leader around the time Yeltsin and the Russians kicked out the Communists. A lot of information and documents fell into the wrong hands, and before you knew it, we had an evil-twin thing happening."

"But—"

"I was wiped off the map, Princess, and I wasn't the only one. I lost everything. Without an iden-tity, I had no money, no friends, nothing. I couldn't access PAX, because they'd buried a body they be-lieved was mine, and closed out my file."

"The ATM," she said softly. "The stolen car. The credit cards."

"You make me sound like a real nice guy," he said ruefully. "I keep records. I'm going to pay it all back one day."

She looked down at her hands as she tried to absorb it all. "The strange thing is, I believe you."

"All of it?"

"All of it." She met his eyes, and a small smile played at the edges of her mouth. "Am I a fool, or what?"

"There's more."

"I think I've heard enough, if it's all the same to you."

His grin was ironic and, she noted, terribly sad. "Sorry, but this is the big one."

She studied his face. "I'm not going to like this one, am I?"

He reached across and brushed a lock of hair from her cheek. "No," he said, "you're not going to like it much at all, but you have to know."

He told her about the altered microchip, and the life they had planned for him.

"Something happened after I died," he said, aware of how fantastic and unbelievable the whole thing sounded. "It took them as much by surprise as it did me. The doctors said it had something to do with the microchip, that it did something to my neurons or whatever, but the bottom line is, I suddenly could lay my hands on someone and heal them.''

She wasn't laughing at him. He was grateful for that. "It hurts you," she said. "You seemed in agony when you put your hands on the bruises on my arms.''

"It's no walk in the park," he said lightly. "But what happened with you is something different.''

"How different?" she asked warily.

"It's pretty simple," he said. "Why heal if you can destroy? They've found a way to jolt the microchip on command.''

"Oh, God," she breathed, knowing what he was about to say.

"You got it, Princess. The perfect crime. No mess, no fuss. Just lay your hands on your victim and watch him die right before your very eyes.''

Her head spun with the enormity of it all. "There has to be some way to change this," she said. "Why don't you just have the chip removed?''

"Right," he said dryly. "I have no identification, no health insurance, and no fingerprints. Can you imagine me walking into a hospital and saying, 'I can't pay you and I can't explain what it's doing there, but how about removing this little microchip I have embedded in my rib cage.'" He looked at her and shook his head. "Somehow I don't think it would fly.''

"I can't accept this," she said. If she accepted it, she would lose hope, and right now hope was all she had.

"That's why I didn't want this to happen between us." His voice was tender, infinitely sad. "You've been hurt enough. It's time you got on with your life."

Tears welled up, and she blinked her eyes rapidly. "We're not going to have our happy ending, are we?"

"Somehow I don't think we are, Princess."

They were quiet for a time. Beyond the window, the sky was growing light.

"I'll bring it down at a field outside of London. I know someplace where you'll be safe."

"I'm coming with you."

"No."

"I have a score to settle with Lucky."

"There's no guarantee I'll find him." And no guarantee that if he did, Lucky would be alive. Whether or not she realized it, she loved her father. He wanted to spare her whatever he could.

"We're in this together, Trask."

"I thought you understood." He forced himself to sound as harsh as the situation in which they found themselves. "There's no happy ending."

"My life," she said. "My choice."

"Not this time."

"You can't stop me."

"Yes," he said slowly, "I can." He'd leave her at the home of people he'd befriended while on the run, and then he'd head for Switzerland and the clinic, where he had the feeling he would find Lucky.

She opened her mouth and was about to argue, but just then he muttered a curse and began scanning instruments and maneuvering dials. "Is something wrong?"

"We're off course," he said, a note of disbelief in his voice.

"That happens," she said easily. "Just make a correction."

"I don't mean a little off course. I mean, we're off the map."

She peered out the window and could barely make out a rocky coastline and lots of turbulent gray water. "Is that the North Sea?"

"Looks like it."

She looked over at him. "Scotland?"

"Scotland."

"So turn around," she said, trying to hide her nerves.

"We've got a bigger problem."

Her heart hammered against her rib cage. "Fuel?"

"We're running real low. I don't think we can make it back to London."

"It's not like Scotland's the end of the earth," she said. "They have airports."

"Not one close enough," he said, his words clipped and urgent. He checked his gauges, eyeballed the terrain below, then checked his gauges again. He knew that island beckoning to him from below. He knew it like the back of his hand.

A setup? he wondered. Was it possible the whole damn thing was part of Viktor's grand scheme?

"Fasten your seat belt," he said. "We're going in for a landing."

Some work's been done on this, he thought as he brought the plane down. The runway was longer than he remembered, and smoother.

"Look!" Martie pointed out the starboard window. "Is that a castle?"

"McLaren Castle," he said, powering down.

"It looks deserted."

"It isn't."

She turned away from the window and met his eyes. "Lucky?"

"Maybe."

"And he's not alone?"

"Right again."

She clasped her hands tightly together to keep from trembling. "You don't seem very surprised."

He wasn't. He was scared. Reaching under his seat, he pulled out her gun, then handed it to her.

"You think I'm going to need this?"

"Yes. If anyone approaches the plane, shoot them."

"I won't be in the plane, Trask," she said slowly. "I'll be with you."

"Too dangerous."

"It's not your decision."

"The hell it's not. I know what's going down, Princess. You don't stand a chance against—"

"Shut up and listen to me."

His jaw dropped. *"What?"*

"You heard me. Too many decisions about my life have been made behind my back. Like it or not, I'm with you on this. It's my life. It's about time I took control of what happens."

"You're going to hear things you don't like in there, Princess."

She wondered if she would ever get the chance to tell him everything that was in her heart...or to hear him say, *I love you.* "I'm not afraid," she said. "Not if I'm with you."

"I should've left you back in Texas," he said. "If anything happens to you—"

"Nothing will happen to me," she said. "You can't tell me we've come this far to lose each other now." He'd been part of her every waking moment for so long, the fabric of her dreams at night. "Don't you know that whatever happens, I want to be with you?"

"I can't guarantee what I'll do in there," he continued, watching her intently. He swallowed, and her heart ached for them both. "I want you to promise me you'll use that gun, if you need to."

She nodded. It was the best she could manage, with the lump of emotion lodged in her throat.

"On me, if you have to."

"Trask, no! I—"

He pulled her close, suddenly starved for the touch and smell of her. Her mouth was sweet and hot, and he wished with all his heart that the end would come swiftly and that when it was over, she would still be alive. She was everything good and beautiful in a dark and ugly world. The fact that she had loved him once proved his soul wasn't so dark, that his empty life wasn't so irredeemable. It proved that even he could be touched by an angel.

The words rose up from the deepest part of his soul, borne on wings of lonliness and longing.

"God, Martie, I lo—"

"Don't say it," she whispered urgently, placing her finger against his lips. "If you say it now, I won't be able to stand it."

"We might not have another chance. You have to know that—"

"I do know," she said, "but I want you to tell me when this is all over."

The words he longed to say tore at his heart. She didn't know what she was asking of him, but then, she still didn't realize he was going to die. Despite it all, she believed there'd be a happy ending for them, that the force of love was greater than any evil man might concoct.

If only he could believe it, too.

They walked toward the castle in silence. The only sound was the relentless crashing of the waves against the rocky shore below. The castle loomed before them, even more ramshackle up close than it had seemed from the plane. It was a moody, melancholy place that made you think of murder plots and dead kings and things that went bump in the night.

The front door was open.

"Convenient," Trask muttered.

They stepped inside. Somehow it was colder in the shelter of the main hall than it had been outside. It smelled musty and damp, as if it hadn't been dry for centuries. They hesitated, unsure which way to go, when a tall man in a dark blue suit seemed to appear from nowhere.

"You will follow me," he said, then turned left and walked down the dark hall.

"Stay behind me," he whispered. "Take note of where we are and how to get back out." She might need it later.

The man in the blue suit stopped before a towering archway. "In here," he said, gesturing for them to step inside.

As dark as it had been in the hallway, that was how bright it was in the huge chamber. Harsh light flooded the room from huge leaded-glass windows that rose from the stone floor to the curved ceiling.

But Martie barely registered any of it. All she saw was her father, gagged and tied to a chair in the center of the room. She'd never seen him so helpless and alone before. Not even in the hospital, after his heart attack, had he looked so vulnerable. Her heart ached with sadness and love, but she pushed back those emotions.

There was no excuse for what he'd done. He should have allowed her to choose her own path, make her own mistakes.

Trask scanned the room. He noted Lucky's position, the man standing in the doorway, the fact that a tiny camera mounted in the far corner of the room was recording everything they said and did.

Lucky looked from Martie to Trask, and Trask felt a sensation of loss so profound it almost knocked him flat. *We're going to lose this time, Lucky. The biggest battle of them all, and we blew it.*

Viktor intended to kill Martie. That was the one sure thing in the entire scenario. If Viktor wanted to destroy Lucky and punish Trask, he'd hit the jackpot with this plan, and Trask had the sickening feeling that Viktor would use him as the lethal weapon.

Chapter Fifteen

"Welcome," said the slim older man in the obviously hand-tailored suit. "We are pleased you chose to join the festivities."

The hairs on the back of Martie's neck rose. Evil, she thought. She was looking into the face of pure evil.

"We hate to inconvenience you in any way," the man went on, "but security is most important." He gestured toward the lackey who'd led them into the chamber. "My assistant will perform the necessary search."

The lackey didn't find anything on Trask, but he would the second he reached Martie. The muscles in her neck and shoulders tightened painfully, and she struggled to maintain her composure. Lucky's eyes never left her.

The lackey stepped in front of her. "Madame," he said, baring his teeth in a grim smile. "If you will allow me—"

"No." The well-dressed older man stepped between them. "It is not necessary."

She didn't dare meet Trask's eyes. Her relief would be too obvious.

"We both know I'm what you want," Trask said, all menace and muscle, as he towered over the smaller man. "Let them go, and I'll stay behind."

"Such arrogance," said the man. "One of the least attractive traits you Americans possess. This is exactly the triumvirate I had long planned to entertain."

"He's a sick old man, Viktor," Trask said, gesturing toward Lucky. "He's out of the loop. What good can he do you now?"

Viktor's eyes, a cold and forbidding aqua, glittered. "He doesn't know," he said to Lucky, who was struggling against his bonds. "This is more than I'd hoped."

"Then let *her* go," Trask said, positioning himself in front of Martie like a human shield. "She doesn't know a damn thing about any of this."

Viktor's expression softened as he looked at her, and Martie felt her stomach knot with apprehension. He dismissed his henchmen, telling them to wait in the anteroom, that he would summon them if needed.

"Sit down, my dear." He gestured toward a Queen Anne chair that stood by the window, an odd sight in the otherwise barren room.

"I'd rather stand, thank you."

"Willful," he observed. "But that can be changed."

A harsh growl issued from Lucky as he tried to make himself heard through the gag. He looked so gray, so ashen, the way he had right after his heart attack. *Oh, God,* she thought. *Daddy!* A fierce protective instinct rose up inside her, pushing everything else away, all of the years of misunderstandings and pain. She started to move toward her father, but Viktor blocked her way.

"Leave her alone," Trask ordered. "She's nothing to you."

"There you are wrong," said Viktor. "She is everything."

"How ridiculous," said Martie. Her heart was pounding so hard she could barely hear her own words. "We've never met."

"I knew you many years ago," said Viktor, "when you were an infant in your mother's arms."

Lucky's inarticulate cries sent a chill up her spine. *What are they doing to you, Daddy?* "I'm afraid I don't remember."

"I held you when you cried."

Involuntarily she turned toward Lucky. "Oh, God!" she cried as her father, still tied to the chair, toppled forward and crashed to the ground. Sweat poured from his forehead, and even from this distance she could see he was having trouble breathing.

She started toward Lucky's side as Trask ran to help his mentor, but Viktor held her fast.

"Let me go!" she cried. "That's my father!"

"No, he isn't," said Viktor. "I am."

"What?" She tried to break his grip, but he was wiry, and very strong. "I don't know what you're talking about."

"We have the same eyes, my dear. My mother's eyes." He smiled that chilly smile. "Your grandmother's eyes."

"You're crazy," she said, even as she saw herself in the shape of his chin, the lift of his brow. "I don't believe a word you're saying."

"Ah, but you do," said Viktor. "Somehow you know I'm telling the truth."

Trask was bent low over Lucky. He untied the gag and tossed it aside. *He's dying,* she thought numbly. The man who had taught her to ride a bicycle and dried her tears when her hamster died. The man who had loved her and nurtured her and only wanted the best for her. She knew in her bones that Viktor would not let Lucky leave this room alive.

"Your mother was my wife," Viktor was saying as Trask administered CPR to Lucky. "You are our child."

"Liar!" She couldn't keep the fear from her voice. "Why are you doing this? You're nothing to me. What could you possibly stand to gain from it?"

"I want what belongs to me." He took her hand in his. "I have watched you over the years, waiting for the right time."

"I don't believe a word you're saying. My birth parents were from New York."

Viktor's laugh was harsh as he glanced quickly toward Lucky, who had regained consciousness. "So that is what he told you, is it? Lie after lie. The fabric of your life is woven from his lies."

She thought of the ten years she'd lost, years when she and Trask could have been together, building a family of their own, and a sense of anger and desolation swept over her with the fierceness of the waves crashing below. Lucky had almost ruined her life with his lies, but she finally understood that his mistakes had been made out of love. The man who stood before her was incapable of the emotion.

She met Viktor's eyes. "You were married to my mother?"

"A beautiful woman," said Viktor in his accented English. He gestured toward Lucky, who was sitting up with Trask's assistance. "He destroyed it all for me with his lies."

"How?" Martie asked. "Did they have an affair?"

Viktor's face turned ugly, and she felt cold all the way through to her marrow. "Yes." The word carried with it years of bitterness. "All those years he kept you from me are unforgivable."

But Lucky did it because he loved you . . . he did it to keep you safe from harm.

Viktor studied her face for what seemed an eternity. She thanked God he didn't have a lie detector handy, only an odd silver box—possibly a tape recorder—clipped to his breast pocket. "You will spend some time with me, Martina. We have many years to account for, many stories to tell."

"No!" Lucky's voice ripped through the air. "Don't listen to him, darlin'!"

"My old friend is dead," Viktor said calmly. "He had his time. Now it is mine."

"You're insane," Martie cried. "He isn't dead. Lucky's alive."

"Martie." Trask's voice rose above hers. "It's serious."

She felt torn in a million directions, fragmented and uncertain. "What's wrong?" she asked, turning toward Trask, her heart thundering.

"Chest pain. Nausea. Pain down his left arm."

"Oh, God . . ." she breathed. "Another heart attack."

"I will call for help," Viktor said smoothly. "Do not worry about Lucky Wilde."

"You bastard," Lucky snarled, in a thin, strained voice. "To hell with me. My time is over. Tell her the *whole* story before I die. Tell her, Viktor. Tell her how you—"

"Enough!" Viktor turned on Lucky, the force of his hatred almost another presence in the room. "Your day is done, old friend."

"Kill me," Lucky taunted, struggling to his feet. He looked like a man on the verge of death. A man with nothing to lose. "Do it, you bastard. Show Martina what you're all about."

Viktor's aqua eyes glittered with a dangerous light. "You tempt me, Lucky Wilde. Almost beyond endurance."

Trask stood behind Lucky. *Why don't you do something?* she thought. *Why are you just standing there?*

Lucky turned toward Martie, and in his eyes she saw love and fear, and her own heart threatened to break in two. He'd made mistakes, they both had, but he loved her as much as she loved him. How on earth could she have ever doubted that?

"Listen to me, darlin'. If you don't hear another word I say, hear this."

"Quiet, old man," Viktor warned. "This is—"

"He killed your ma. Crept into her studio while you slept up at the big house, and strangled her with his bare hands."

"No," she said, thinking of the beautiful young mother she'd loved. "Don't say it, Daddy, please don't say it." She couldn't bear the thought that her mother's last moments had been filled with terror at the hands of someone she knew.

"It's true, darlin'." He rubbed his left arm, as if to ease the pain. "We thought she was finally safe from him, that we'd buried the traces, but—"

"Stop!" she cried, clapping her hands over her ears. "I don't want to hear this."

"You *must* hear it!" Lucky cried, with all the strength he could muster. "He killed your mama in cold blood, and he'll do the same to—"

With that, Lucky fell to the side. Trask caught him just before he hit the ground.

"Ask him," Lucky managed, his voice almost inaudible. "Ask him for the truth, darlin'—"

"Is it true?" Martie whirled around to face Viktor. "Did you kill my mother?"

"She was an unfaithful bitch," Viktor said coldly. "All that mattered was the child." Again that arctic smile. *"You."*

"That's not the whole story, Martie," Trask said. "During the pregnancy, every time your mother tried to leave him, he threatened to kill the unborn baby...you." Lucky had offered her a haven—and something even more wonderful. He'd offered her love.

"You knew?" she asked Trask. "You've always known?"

"Lucky told me the day I left." Lucky had been in the process of cutting ties with PAX. Allowing his daughter to marry a PAX operative would have been tantamount to signing her death warrant. There would no longer be any way he could protect her from Viktor's influence.

Tears burned her eyes, blurring her vision. "It's true?" she asked Viktor, horrified. "You killed my mother?" She'd been told Marta had died suddenly of an aneurysm. Swift and silent and painless. How she wished she still believed that.

"The past is done," said Viktor, dismissing his actions with a wave of his hand, "or will be very soon. We have the future to consider. There is much I can offer you, Martina. So much more than Lucky Wilde ever could."

Lucky groaned and clutched at his chest.

Trask cradled her father in his arms.

"Oh, God, do something!" Martie cried. "Please, do something for him!"

The expression of despair on Trask's face spoke volumes. Especially to Viktor.

"Quite a dilemma, isn't it, my boy?" Viktor obviously relished the situation. "I could call someone to help him, but I have heard you are quite gifted in these matters.''

What on earth was he talking about? All Trask had to do was lay his hands on Lucky, and—

"No," she whispered, remembering what Trask had told her as they flew through the night. "It's not fair...." Viktor's side had developed a way to turn Trask's healing abilities into something darker, more sadistic, and she realized that no matter what Trask chose to do, Lucky was doomed.

"If you don't help him, he will most assuredly die," Viktor said calmly, watching the scene with avid interest. "And yet, if you *do* choose to lend aid and comfort—" he fingered the silver box hanging from his breast pocket "—I might find a way to end the poor man's suffering."

Rivers of sweat poured down Lucky's face and neck, and his hands were tightly clenched into fists. His breathing was shallow, and she could see that his pulse was as rapid as a jackhammer.

"Are you a gambling man, Benedict?" Viktor asked. "Will you take the chance?"

FOR TWO YEARS time had been Trask's enemy.

Now it looked as if time were going to win the battle after all.

Across the room, Martie looked at him with an expression of such anguish, such indescribable pain, that he would have given anything to be able to erase it from her heart and mind, if only that were possible.

Back in Texas, in that cheap motel room, he'd believed anything was possible. For a little while, with the woman he'd loved and lost and lived to find again, he'd let himself think about a future. About a home of his own. About the family, a *real* family, that he'd never had.

All they needed was a lousy ten minutes more, six hundred seconds more, and he could have the happily-ever-after ending he'd never have believed possible in a thousand lifetimes, not just the two he'd been granted. But it was over now. Martie's heart, her beautiful, innocent heart, had been cut in two by Viktor and, God help them, they'd all played a part.

Secrets. Too damned many secrets. And now those secrets were going to put an end to his life and to Lucky's. His gut twisted as he thought of Martie. Viktor had done his worst to her already. In ten minutes, PAX operatives would reach the shore and scale the cliffs to McLaren Castle, and she would be saved.

Lucky had said the magic word and managed to pull off one more miracle, but this time the miracle would come too late.

For Lucky.

For Trask.

For the future he and Martie could have shared.

He tore his gaze from Martie and looked down at the man who'd been a father to him. The only person on earth, other than Martie, who'd given a damn whether he lived or died, whether he built a good life or spent his time in the shadows. Lucky's face was sheet-white. His lips were going cyanotic.

It was now or never.

He laid his hands on the man's chest, fingers splayed over the breastbone. "Let go," he murmured as he waited for the pain to come to him. "Let it all go, Lucky...let it all go—"

"No!" Lucky roused himself from his pain, the word barely audible.

A deep sense of sadness flooded Trask, but he let it wash over him and away. He needed to concentrate, to pour his entire being into the task at hand. Vaguely he was aware of Martie, the sound of her voice, Viktor's rolling tenor rising above it in anger and pleading. He knew they didn't have a chance in hell of getting out of this alive and together, but he couldn't let that stop him. They'd all come too far for that.

"It's out of your hands, Lucky," he said to the man struggling beneath his hands.

"Martie—"

"Save your strength. You're going to need it when we try to escape."

Lucky probably didn't believe that was possible any more than Trask did, but this wasn't exactly the time for negative thinking.

Closing his eyes, he willed himself deeper into Lucky's pain, into the darkness, down through the abyss...

MARTIE FELT as if she were suspended in time and space, floating free through a dark void of terror.

This couldn't be happening. Less than two days ago, she'd been on her way to her engagement party, worrying about runs in her panty hose. Now she was standing next to her birth father in a tumbledown castle off the coast of Scotland, watching the man she loved try to save the life of the only real father she'd ever known.

A low, growling moan came from Trask. His face was contorted with pain, but still he kept his hands pressed against Lucky's chest. It was hard to see through her tears but Lucky's color seemed better, not quite so ashen.

Was it possible—could there be any chance at all that Viktor was bluffing, that this was just a sadistic exercise in playing with their emotions? *Please, God,* she prayed. *Just a little more time.*

Viktor shifted position next to her. Her gaze was riveted to Trask and Lucky, but her peripheral vision was acute. She turned slightly and saw Viktor's slim, elegant hand curved around the silver box that hung from his breast pocket. His index finger was poised over a round button on top.

The reversal process.

Viktor was going to do it. He was going to push that button and kill Lucky right there in front of her, kill him as if Lucky were nothing but a garden slug beneath his fancy shoes. She felt dizzy with fear.

She wasn't foolish enough to believe she could fight him for the silver box. His lackeys would be all over her in a millisecond, and she would probably lose both Lucky and Trask in the bargain.

But there was something she could do.

She reached into the waistband of her jeans, beneath the oversize sweater, and pulled out her gun. She'd fought Lucky tooth and nail about getting a gun, but he'd made a persuasive case, and she'd promised to at least carry the gun when she was transporting expensive pieces of jewelry.

Who could have known it would be her last chance to save his life?

She aimed the gun at Viktor. It took him a moment to realize what she was about.

"Do not be hasty," he said, his sangfroid incredible, considering the fact a loaded pistol was pointed at his head. "I am merely an observer."

"Do not lie to me," she said, mocking his words. "Take your hand away from that silver box and do it slowly."

"This?" He glanced down at the apparatus hooked to his breast pocket. "This is only a cigarette case."

"You're a liar," she said, trying to match his ice with fire. "I know what that is. Give it to me."

"I am your father," Viktor said, his eyes not leaving hers.

"No," she said loudly, for the world to hear. "Lucky Wilde is my father."

"My seed gave you life."

"You are nothing to me." She spat on the ground at his feet. "You killed my mother."

"There is much you need to know."

"I know everything I want to know about you. Give me that box or, so help me, I'll kill you."

"There is a softness in your eyes, Martina. You lack the resolve."

What a fool you are, she thought. Lucky had never doubted just how strong she really was.

She heard Trask's voice and—thank you, God, thank you a thousand times—Lucky's, as well, but she didn't dare turn around. "The count of ten, Viktor, and I count fast."

He moved toward her.

Do it, Martie, do it do it do it do it—

You lack the guts, his eyes taunted. *You will take the path of least resistance.*

Now, Martie, now!

Her finger curled around the trigger.

"Give me the gun, Martie," Trask said, racing toward her. "Let me finish the son of a bitch off."

"He's mine," she said, in a voice she barely recognized, "and he's going to die."

"Perhaps," said Viktor, "but I will not die alone."

He was going to do it, push that button and—

Before she could pull the trigger, a blast echoed off the walls as a bullet pierced Viktor's hand-tailored suit and found its mark where a heart should have been. Both Trask and Martie spun around to find Lucky standing in the middle of the room, holding a smoking gun.

"Sorry for buttin' in, children," said Lucky Wilde with a tired smile, "but that one was mine."

Viktor's body fell to the floor, but nobody noticed.

All Martie could see was that the man she loved and the father she adored were still alive. She flew across the room to where Lucky stood, just as his legs gave out. He sagged against her, and she welcomed the burden.

"You're my girl," Lucky said, love and pride shining from his tired eyes. "So proud of you—"

She cradled him against her. "You're going to be fine, Daddy," she said. "I promise you that."

Trask knelt down beside her father. "He's dead, Lucky. You don't have to worry any longer."

Lucky's eyes closed for a moment, and Martie saw a tear trickle down his cheek. "You two..." He struggled with his words. "Hang on to each other... It all goes by so fast—"

"Quiet," said Trask, with a wink for Martie. "Let me take care of things."

He laid his hands upon her father's chest, and Martie watched as love performed one more miracle.

Epilogue

Change everything, except your loves.
—Voltaire

It was a great night for flying.

The sky over McLaren Castle was a deep, velvety black blanketed with stars that twinkled like a cascade of flawless diamonds.

Martie chuckled softly as she leaned her head back against the plush seat and closed her eyes. No doubt about it: She was her father's daughter.

"You're laughing." Trask took the seat next to her. Dark circles rimmed his eyes. The crescent-shaped scar on his cheek stood out in bold relief against his pale face. She had never seen a more beautiful sight in her entire life.

"I just realized something wonderful," she said, as he took her hand in his and kissed her palm. "I couldn't be more Lucky's daughter if his blood ran through my veins."

"I've always known that, Princess."

"I wish I had," she said softly. "So much wasted time..."

"He would have done anything to keep you safe."

She nodded, finding it hard to speak around the lump in her throat. "Has his plane taken off?"

Trask nodded. "The doctors said he's stable and doing fine, but I don't think any of us will relax until they get him to the hospital in London."

Lucky had, indeed, suffered a massive heart attack, but thanks to Trask's miraculous ability, most of the damage had been healed.

As a precaution, Lucky was being flown to the hospital in a special PAX plane that had been outfitted as an airborne intensive care unit.

"I think we've used up our share of miracles for one lifetime," Martie said, leaning her head against Trask's shoulder.

"You're wrong," he said, lifting her chin so that she met his eyes. "Every day that we're together is a miracle."

They'd defied every obstacle fate had managed to throw in their path, including death, and still they were together.

And still they loved.

A pleasant-faced member of the flight crew appeared before them. "Please fasten your seat belts, folks. The pilot said we'll be taking off any minute." He vanished forward into the cockpit of the private jet as the plane began to roll toward the makeshift runway.

Martie peered out the window as she snapped her seat belt closed. "The castle looks beautiful in the moonlight," she mused. All moody and magnificent, with the silvery sea billowing around it. "I hope I never have to see it again as long as I live."

Trask winced. "I wish you hadn't said that."

"Why?" she asked, perplexed. "I can't imagine you have much affection for the place, either."

"Actually, I have more affection for it than you might think." He looked at her, a sheepish expression on his face. "I own it."

She swatted him on the arm with a cocktail napkin. "Sure you do."

"Seriously." He grinned at her. "My mother left it to me in her will."

"In her will?" Martie couldn't hide her astonishment. She'd always imagined him to have come from a rough-and-tumble blue-collar background.

"McLaren Publishing," he said.

Her jaw dropped. "You're joking."

He shook his head. "And my father was Benedict Books."

"You're rich!"

"Yep," he said, nodding. "Actually, I'm filthy rich." Or he would be, once he got the ticklish matter of personal identification straightened out. He grinned. "Probably a hell of a lot richer than you, come to think of it."

"Wow," said Martie dryly. "I had no idea I was marrying you for your money."

His dark brows lifted. "Marrying me? Who said anything about marriage?"

"I did," said Martie, with the supreme confidence of a woman who knew she was well loved and who loved well in return. "You realize I'll be cut out of my inheritance if I don't get married, and I can't let that happen."

"Do I have any say in this?"

"No," she said blithely. "Now it's my turn to make the decisions, and I've decided that we're going to be married."

"People are going to talk, Princess."

She waved her hand in the air. "Let 'em."

"You're going to get a reputation."

"Wonderful! I've always wanted a reputation."

"Another engagement party?" he asked, his hazel eyes dancing with delight.

"Even bigger this time," she said, warming up to the subject. "We'll invite everyone in the entire state. Black tie and tails and expensive gifts are mandatory."

"What about old Jason Blackburn?" he asked. "He's not going to be real happy with this turn of events."

She grinned like the Cheshire cat. "I doubt if Jason will even notice."

Trask frowned. "I'm not going to have him pop up in church on our wedding day and stake a claim."

"Don't worry," said Martie. "I called home while you were talking to one of those PAX people on the runway. Jason eloped yesterday with Mindy Richardson." The daughter of the bigwig Jason had been so tickled to meet the night of their engagement party.

They looked at each other and started to laugh.

"I love you," he said, and she heard the sound of forever in his words.

"I've waited a long time to hear that, Trask Benedict," she whispered as tears filled her eyes. "A very long time."

He smiled back at her, a happy man.

But Martie wasn't quite finished with him yet. She extended her left hand and wiggled her fingers under his nose. "I tossed away a seven-carat diamond for this moment, Benedict. You'd better find something for this ring finger, and fast!"

He reached down the neck of his T-shirt and pulled out the silver chain with the zircon ring suspended from it. Quickly he unhooked the chain and slipped off the ring.

Trembling with nerves, she extended her left hand. He kissed the palm and each fingertip in turn. Joy exploded inside her like the birth of a star as he slipped the silver ring onto the proper finger.

It was too heavy and too big by half, but she couldn't imagine anything more fitting.

"Marry me, Princess." His rough-honey voice was urgent with emotion. "We've wasted enough time. Let's make those promises and take those vows and start the biggest, most beautiful family in the state of Texas."

"We'll live in Texas?" she asked with a grin.

"We'll live in Texas."

"And we'll have six kids?"

"Eight, if you're willing."

"And you'll love me until the day I die?"

"I'll love you in this life and the next, Princess. You're my heart and my soul and the reason for every breath I take, and if I can see your beautiful face on the pillow next to me every morning for the next sixty years, I'll consider myself a lucky man. So what do you say, Princess? Will you marry me?"

She whispered three words in his ear, and his face lit up with a smile that made her heart sing.

"Yeah?" he asked, clearly delighted.

"Yeah," she said, clearly pleased. "And now that it's official, will you do me a favor?"

"Anything, Princess. Name it, and it's yours."

"Oh, Trask," she said, throwing herself into his arms. "Will you just shut up and kiss me?"

HARLEQUIN™

A M E R I C A N ✦ R O M A N C E®

In Name Only

With the advent of spring, American Romance is pleased to be presenting exciting couples, each with their own unique reasons for needing a new beginning...for needing to enter into a marriage of convenience.

In April we brought you #580 MARRIAGE INCORPORATED by Debbi Rawlins, and in May we offered #583 THE RUNAWAY BRIDE by Jacqueline Diamond. Next, meet the reluctant newlyweds in:

#587 A SHOTGUN WEDDING
Cathy Gillen Thacker
June 1995

Find out why some couples marry first...and learn to love later. Watch for the upcoming "In Name Only" promotion.

INO-3

HARLEQUIN®

AMERICAN ◆ ROMANCE®

Once in a while, there's a story so special, a story so unusual,
that your pulse races, your blood rushes. We call this

AMERICAN
ROMANCE

heart
beat

THE COWBOY & THE BELLY DANCER is one such book.

When rancher Parker Dunlap acquired guardianship of his niece and nephew, he got
a beautiful woman in the bargain! Trouble was, she said her name was Nesrin and
claimed she'd appeared out of a brass lamp! She was a genius with kids and a great
kisser—but was she a marriage-minded genie?

THE COWBOY & THE BELLY DANCER
by
Charlotte Maclay

Available in June wherever Harlequin books are sold. Watch for more Heartbeat
stories, coming your way soon!

ANNOUNCING THE

FLYAWAY VACATION SWEEPSTAKES!

This month's destination:

Beautiful SAN FRANCISCO!

This month, as a special surprise, we're offering an exciting FREE VACATION!

Think how much fun it would be to visit San Francisco "on us"! You could ride cable cars, visit Chinatown, see the Golden Gate Bridge and dine in some of the finest restaurants in America!

The facing page contains two Entry Coupons (as does every book you received this shipment). Complete and return *all* the entry coupons; **the more times you enter, the better your chances of winning!**

Then keep your fingers crossed, because you'll find out by June 15, 1995 if you're the winner! If you are, here's what you'll get:

- Round-trip airfare for two to beautiful San Francisco!
- 4 days/3 nights at a first-class hotel!
- $500.00 pocket money for meals and sightseeing!

Remember: The more times you enter, the better your chances of winning!*

FLYAWAY VACATION
SWEEPSTAKES
OFFICIAL ENTRY COUPON

This entry must be received by: MAY 30, 1995
This month's winner will be notified by: JUNE 15, 1995
Trip must be taken between: JULY 30, 1995-JULY 30, 1996

YES, I want to win the San Francisco vacation for two. I understand the prize
includes round-trip airfare, first-class hotel and $500.00 spending money.
Please let me know if I'm the winner!

Name_____

Address _____ Apt. _____

City   State/Prov.   Zip/Postal Code

Account #_____

Return entry with invoice in reply envelope.

© 1995 HARLEQUIN ENTERPRISES LTD.   CSF KAL

FLYAWAY VACATION
SWEEPSTAKES
OFFICIAL ENTRY COUPON

This entry must be received by: MAY 30, 1995
This month's winner will be notified by: JUNE 15, 1995
Trip must be taken between: JULY 30, 1995-JULY 30, 1996

YES, I want to win the San Francisco vacation for two. I understand the prize
includes round-trip airfare, first-class hotel and $500.00 spending money.
Please let me know if I'm the winner!

Name_____

Address _____ Apt. _____

City   State/Prov.   Zip/Postal Code

Account #_____

Return entry with invoice in reply envelope.

© 1995 HARLEQUIN ENTERPRISES LTD.   CSF KAL

OFFICIAL RULES
FLYAWAY VACATION SWEEPSTAKES 3449
NO PURCHASE OR OBLIGATION NECESSARY

Three Harlequin Reader Service 1995 shipments will contain respectively, coupons for entry into three different prize drawings, one for a trip for two to San Francisco, another for a trip for two to Las Vegas and the third for a trip for two to Orlando, Florida. To enter any drawing using an Entry Coupon, simply complete and mail according to directions.

There is no obligation to continue using the Reader Service to enter and be eligible for any prize drawing. You may also enter any drawing by hand printing the words "Flyaway Vacation," your name and address on a 3"x5" card and the destination of the prize you wish that entry to be considered for (i.e., San Francisco trip, Las Vegas trip or Orlando trip). Send your 3"x5" entries via first-class mail (limit: one entry per envelope) to: Flyaway Vacation Sweepstakes 3449, c/o Prize Destination you wish that entry to be considered for, P.O. Box 1315, Buffalo, NY 14269-1315, USA or P.O. Box 610, Fort Erie, Ontario L2A 5X3, Canada.

To be eligible for the San Francisco trip, entries must be received by 5/30/95; for the Las Vegas trip, 7/30/95; and for the Orlando trip, 9/30/95.

Winners will be determined in random drawings conducted under the supervision of D.L. Blair, Inc., an independent judging organization whose decisions are final, from among all eligible entries received for that drawing. San Francisco trip prize includes round-trip airfare for two, 4-day/3-night weekend accommodations at a first-class hotel, and $500 in cash (trip must be taken between 7/30/95—7/30/96, approximate prize value—$3,500); Las Vegas trip includes round-trip airfare for two, 4-day/3-night weekend accommodations at a first-class hotel, and $500 in cash (trip must be taken between 9/30/95—9/30/96, approximate prize value—$3,500); Orlando trip includes round-trip airfare for two, 4-day/3-night weekend accommodations at a first-class hotel, and $500 in cash (trip must be taken between 11/30/95—11/30/96, approximate prize value—$3,500). All travelers must sign and return a Release of Liability prior to travel. Hotel accommodations and flights are subject to accommodation and schedule availability. Sweepstakes open to residents of the U.S. (except Puerto Rico) and Canada, 18 years of age or older. Employees and immediate family members of Harlequin Enterprises, Ltd., D.L. Blair, Inc., their affiliates, subsidiaries and all other agencies, entities and persons connected with the use, marketing or conduct of this sweepstakes are not eligible. Odds of winning a prize are dependent upon the number of eligible entries received for that drawing. Prize drawing and winner notification for each drawing will occur no later than 15 days after deadline for entry eligibility for that drawing. Limit: one prize to an individual, family or organization. All applicable laws and regulations apply. Sweepstakes offer void wherever prohibited by law. Any litigation within the province of Quebec respecting the conduct and awarding of the prizes in this sweepstakes must be submitted to the Regies des loteries et Courses du Quebec. In order to win a prize, residents of Canada will be required to correctly answer a time-limited arithmetical skill-testing question. Value of prizes are in U.S. currency.

Winners will be obligated to sign and return an Affidavit of Eligibility within 30 days of notification. In the event of noncompliance within this time period, prize may not be awarded. If any prize or prize notification is returned as undeliverable, that prize will not be awarded. By acceptance of a prize, winner consents to use of his/her name, photograph or other likeness for purposes of advertising, trade and promotion on behalf of Harlequin Enterprises, Ltd., without further compensation, unless prohibited by law.

For the names of prizewinners (available after 12/31/95), send a self-addressed, stamped envelope to: Flyaway Vacation Sweepstakes 3449 Winners, P.O. Box 4200, Blair, NE 68009.

RVC KAL